The Legend of Goo-Shu

JOURNAL 1

Story and Illustrations by

Raeshin Kim

First Edition

RK Enterprises, Inc.

Published by
RK Enterprises, Inc.
151 E. Skylark Ct.
Allyn, WA 98524

Copyright 2003

Final design by Seong-hwan Kim

ISBN 0-9743775-0-3

Printed by DaeWoo Printing, South Korea

I dedicate this book to those to whom I have the most reason to thank;
My Mother and Father,
My Wife
And
My baby boy
Thank you for your love,
Your support
And most of all,
For your unending patience
It's been a trial
An agonizing,
Exquisite
And rewarding trial

The Legend of Goo-shu: Journal 1

The World of Goo-shu
391 A.D.

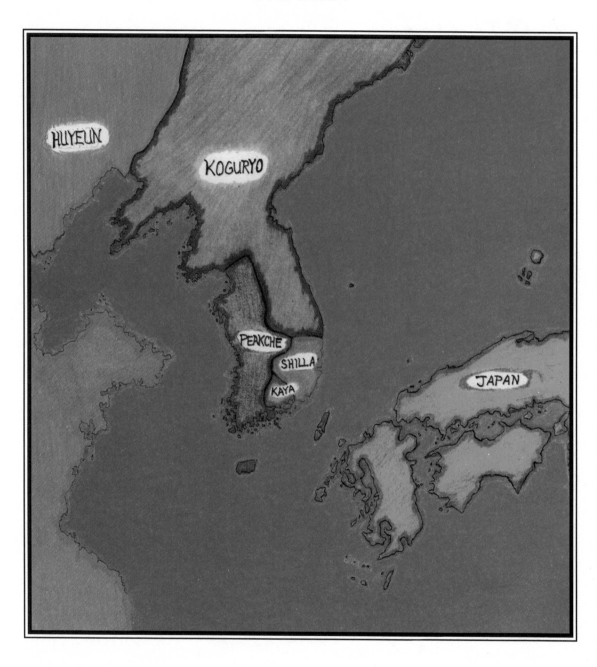

Prologue

Centuries ago, to the north of what is now Kang-won Do province in the country of Korea, there was a narrow valley. The valley was home to two small farming villages. One was situated at the western end of the valley and the other at the east. Life was simple for these rural folk. The seasons came and went and the crops were harvested. Farming was not the easiest way of life, but it was peaceful and everyone was content. All of this ended on a sunny day in early summer.

Two fourteen-year-old boys, one from each village, were out hiking in the mountains that surrounded the valley when they came across the dilapidated

hut of an old hag. The villagers in the valley below knew the hag to be a witch and kept well away from her. The two boys had been told many times not to go near her, because she was both powerful and dangerous. However, the mischievous boys, ignoring the warnings of their village elders, went to the witch's hut and stole her last chicken to eat as an afternoon snack.

Discovering what the boys had done, the witch delved into the blackest of her ancient arts. From her dark magic was brought forth a terrible curse to punish both the boys and their villages. The curse decreed that the two boys, who had worked together to steal and eat her only chicken, would be forced to battle one another for the future of their villages. The losing boy would be turned into a chicken each night

for the rest of his life and his village would suffer seven years of hardship. The victorious boy would keep his human form and his village would know seven years of prosperity.

Should the boys decide not to fight, then both villages would be cursed to suffer for seven years. This dreaded contest would have to be held every seven years on the same day thereafter. To forever chain the villagers to their harsh fate, the witch decreed that anyone who left the valley for more than a few days would likewise suffer the chicken curse. From that day forward, none dared leave the cursed valley.

Eager to spare themselves the witch's wrath, the villagers forced the two reluctant boys to fight. The boy from the Western Village won that first martial contest and for the next seven years, his people prospered. However, that very night, to their horror and dismay, the people of the Eastern Village watched as their failed champion was transformed into a chicken. Seven years of

unrelenting hardship followed. With their crops blighted and livestock sick and dying, the Eastern Villagers fell on the hardest of times. Desperate for food, they came to look upon their defeated chicken boy with angry, hungry eyes. On the seventh anniversary of the first fateful contest, two more fourteen-year old boys were selected to fight.

These new champions had trained hard to win. Their continued humanity, as well as the prosperity of their friends and family, hung in the balance. Honors would be heaped upon the winner, while life in a village full of hungry people with empty stew pots awaited the loser.

This cursed seven-year cycle continued for over a hundred years. During that time, the martial contest and the preparation that went into training new champions came to dominate the relationship between the villages. Friendly, peaceful feelings between the two communities disappeared as each village sought to save itself from the hardships of the old witch's curse at the expense of the other.

It was into this hostile era of village rivalry that the author of this journal was born. His story was not that of a great hero. He was but a simple young man, not possessed of exceptional nobility. Nor did he always act with sound judgment. Rather, it was the wondrous adventures he embarked on that made him special and his story so compelling. The boy's name was Kang Goo-shu, and this is his tale as written by him.

May 18
The Year of the Rabbit

I left my village yesterday just before dusk. Sneaking away as I did was the hardest thing I've ever done. I regretted leaving my home but could see no other alternative. The shame and fear I felt after my humiliating defeat made staying impossible. I couldn't bear to look my family or neighbors in the eye. What worried me most, however, was the way everyone licked their chops as I passed them on the street. They looked at me as if I were a meal with legs rather than their once beloved Goo-shu. The bums! I suppose I can hardly blame them. After all, I had lost the sacred duel. Now the village would suffer for another seven years. As for me, I'm a cursed chicken boy. Parting with everyone and everything I've ever known is merely salt upon this terrible wound.

My awful fate is all the fault of that rotten Shin Young-goo. It's because of him that I'm cursed. That cheating fink tricked me. If it weren't for his treachery, victory would've been mine. I'd have been a

hero and my village would have lived well. Now, thanks to him, I'm looked upon by my family as a failure and, worse still, as the main course for dinner.

I'd trained since I was three-years-old to beat the Western Village's champion. After losing the last contest, we'd suffered badly. The entire village had sacrificed so that I and the other boys in training would be strong and fit. In the end, it was my superior skills that made me the best candidate. I was selected over four other boys my age to represent our village. When the day came for

me to remove the witch's curse from my people, what happens? I fall prey to the treachery of my opponent. The fight was supposed to be a noble duel between worthy adversaries, but that pig butt eating punk, Shin Young-goo, was a dirty little cheat.

This is how it happened.

It's well known by the people of both villages that I have somewhat bad eyesight. It's also common knowledge that I'm the toughest fighter the valley has produced in generations. My powerful body and good looks always inspired and intimidated people.

No boy in the valley was my equal. Everyone said that I was sure to win the upcoming fight. It must have been the total certainty of the beating he was going to suffer at my hands that led Shin Young-goo to do what he did. The spineless coward!

The traditional meeting place for the fight was the central field that separated the farming lands of the Eastern and Western Villages. The contest grounds were bordered on the right by the forest that led into the northern mountains. The wretch Shin Young-goo and I would meet there to do battle.

On the day of destiny, our respective villages gathered at opposite ends of the field. My people and I were the first to arrive. They lined up behind me and chanted my name loudly. Their enthusiasm ran high. All of them, myself included, anticipated a swift victory for me in the upcoming duel.

I looked up and smiled. Overhead, the sky was clear and blue. The sun had passed the midday point and shone warmly on my face. These were good omens. My noble ancestors and the great powers of heaven were surely looking down upon me with kindness and favor. This assumption was soon to be proven wrong.

I strode confidently across the open field and stood at its center, awaiting my unworthy opponent. The edge of the forest was to my right. Shin Young-goo soon arrived at the head of his people. Something about the way he looked was odd. For reasons I didn't at the time understand, the devious coward had dressed himself in clothes that matched the mottled colorings of the shrubs and trees of the forest. He'd even gone so far as to fasten small branches and leaves to his clothing. Had I realized at the time my foe's intent, things would be different for me now. To my eternal shame, the confidence I had in my overwhelmingly superior skills blinded me to just how low the truly desperate will stoop.

Before the duel had even started, Shin Young-goo positioned himself so that the forest was behind him. His clothes blended in perfectly with the background. My weak eyes were unable to distinguish him from the trees. I squinted to see more clearly.

However, it was only when he moved that I could tell Shin Young-goo apart from the green of the forest.

The starting signal of the contest would be a single, thunderous "gong" from the great bull drum of the valley. The drum stood as high

as a man was tall and was made from stretched bull hide. Its sound could be heard throughout the valley.

With the striking of the drum, Shin Young-goo leapt to the attack. He flew at my head with a sloppy jump kick. Despite his disguise, I detected his movement and ducked the kick in time. Repeatedly, I

tried circling the crafty little fink so that the trees would no longer be behind him. Each time I did, Shin Young-goo countered my move.

Shin Young-goo came at me again and again. His punches and kicks whizzed towards me, but my defense was impeccable. I blocked deftly and then counter attacked. My wily foe evaded the more powerful blows I threw at him and in turn punched at my head. Ducking the punch, I shot in and countered with one of my own, a Hurricane Punch to the worm's gut. The wimp was badly stunned and doubled over in pain. In desperation, he reached out to hold on to me so that I couldn't strike him again. The pathetic coward clung to me like stink on sweaty feet. It was an embarrassment to have been paired against such a goat booger.

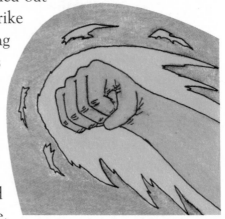

With a shove I pushed Shin Young-goo away and pressed the attack. The forest was still behind him making it difficult to see him and harder still to land a decisive strike.

Nevertheless, most of my blows connected, at least in part. It was obvious by the fool's feeble attempts to defend himself that he'd soon taste the bitter brew of defeat I was preparing to serve him.

Dazed and weakened by my relentless assault, Shin Young-goo almost stumbled over his own feet trying to back away. My mighty blows drove him to the very edge of the woods. Knowing that the moment was totally mine, I surged forward. My excited village cheered me on. Victory was imminent.

Angry shouts and vile curses, directed at the both of us, came from the people of Shin Young-goo's village. The Western Villagers could tell that their pitiful excuse for a champion was about to fall before my peerless might and skill.

Our epic battle had moved into the woods. Staggering back from the awesome power of my Typhoon Kick, Shin Young-goo stood witless and at my mercy. His back was against the trunk of an old tree. All that remained was for me to put an end to the one-sided fight. A single, decisive punch would do it.

The people of both villages cheered and shouted excitedly. They knew that the next moment would decide their fates for the coming seven years. All were waiting for me to act. Unfortunately, instead of finishing off my hapless foe, I first took a second to wave victoriously to my people. Because of my poor vision they appeared as little more than a blur. Still, I knew that my honored parents were among them, looking on proudly. Little did I realize that while my back was turned that weak-kneed Shin Young-goo, so exhausted from the pummeling I'd given him, had fallen to his knees. Not having seen this happen, I turned back to finish off that crusty scab with my Flying Devastator Kick. Aiming at what I thought was his head, I charged in. In my carelessness, though, I mistook the blurry shape of a knot in the tree for Shin Young-goo's homely mug. The crushing power of my kick sent my foot ripping through the bark of the old tree and my leg became imbedded deep in its rotted trunk.

Dangling there by my trapped leg, I struggled desperately to free myself. I could hear my people shouting, yelling at me to do something. Likewise, Shin Young-goo's village called out to him. They urged him to seize the moment.

Responding to the cries of his people, Shin Young-goo made his move. The shameless dog kisser stood back up and smirked at me as I hung there. Then without saying a word, he attacked.

In my vulnerable state, I was unable to offer up a decent defense to the girlie-like blows of Shin Young-goo. Though not powerful in a manly way, the coward kept hitting me, wearing me down with punch after punch, kick after kick. Somewhere between the repeated blows to my head and stomach, I blacked out.

The next thing I remembered was waking up on the ground. I'd fallen free of the tree and lay in a bruised heap on the grass. My parents were standing only a short distance away, their faces riddled with grief and shame. I'd never before seen them so sad. I had to turn away from the painful image. As I did, I saw Shin Young-goo. That disgrace to stinky farts everywhere was being carried off triumphantly on the shoulders of his cheering village.

This could not be happening! I told myself that this was just a nightmare and that I was dreaming. As much as I wanted to believe that none of this was real, I knew that it was. The impossible had happened. I'd been defeated. The fates had conspired against me, robbing me of my deserved victory. Everything in life sucked so bad!

No one spoke to me on the walk back to our village. My parents and siblings shunned me. At this point, I hadn't even thought about the chicken curse or how it would soon change my life so completely. All I could think about was that lowly, dishonorable cheat, Shin Young-goo. He was being applauded as a great hero. He was the savior of his village, while I was lower than dirt in the eyes of mine. This was so unfair. I couldn't imagine things getting any worse.

Once everyone had returned to the village, I began to notice the looks that people gave me. The old men and women stared at me with wide-eyed hunger. This was very unusual behavior even for elderly people. I felt more than a little alarmed by it. I assumed that the time spent out in the hot sun had given everyone great appetites. Oh, what a naïve fool I was.

Our village's previous champion, a boy named Lee Sung-woo, had also lost his duel and brought about the last seven years of hardship. I hadn't known him well. I was only seven-years-old when that contest took place. Sung-woo had run away immediately following his defeat. Or, at least that's what the rest of us boys had been told. As I entered my home, I wondered whether or not I, too, should run away.

My social standing in the community could never be redeemed. I'd never be a hero. I would never again be popular or respected. Up until that day all the girls in the village wanted to walk beside me, hoping I'd hold hands with them. Now, no respectable girl would consider me as a potential husband. Even the village toilet digger's thirty-year-old, single, one-eyed daughter would probably scoff at the thought of marrying me. I was doomed to be hated and alone thanks to Shin Young-goo and my lousy eyesight.

My mother and older sister Mi-young had returned home first. The two were in the kitchen, preparing the evening meal when I arrived. Their mood was glum and their heads were lowered. They sobbed as they readied a fire and brought out the family stew pot.

Still too ashamed to speak to them, I sat on the floor across from the kitchen. I watched as they prepared the vegetables and spices for a stew. As they worked, I noticed the ingredients they were setting out: green onions, meat salts and an assortment of vegetables. It appeared they were preparing to make chicken stew. I found this odd, since we currently had no chickens.

Then it dawned on me. We did have a chicken! Or at least we would in a few hours when the sun went down. The old witch's curse! The chicken curse! According to it, the loser of the duel turned into a chicken at sunset. If indeed this were true, I would become a chicken in only a few hours! I'd been so upset about losing the fight that I had completely forgotten about the parts of the curse that pertained to the failed champion. From the beginning, I was so positive that I would win that I hadn't given any thought to the consequences of defeat.

The people of my village never spoke of the chicken curse directly to the young boys in training, but we knew of it all the same. I'd always regarded it as merely a myth, a ploy the adults used to spur us on in our training and to keep us from straying too far from the village. However, years ago I'd overheard two of the village elders talking about it. They spoke about the curse as though they took it very seriously. Then, of course, there was the fact that no one I knew of, with the exception of Sung-woo, had ever left our valley. Had that been because of the chicken curse too? I remained uncertain. I'd never seen the effects of the curse, as Sung-woo had never returned. Or, had he left at all? Perhaps his family had devoured him? Was my family also preparing to do such an unthinkable thing?

Shock and fear ran through me. I wanted to ask my mother and sister if what I suspected were true. Surely it couldn't be. I knew things had been hard the last seven years and that the difficulties would continue due to my failure but still, I was their beloved Goo-shu. How could I be thought of as dinner?

I listened to the low sobbing of my mother and Mi-young as they worked. I hesitated to bring up my concerns to them, fearing their response. Then my father entered the house. My little brother, Young-seol, was right behind him. Father was quiet and somber. He refused to look at me. As the head of our household, he bore the greatest portion of my dishonor. I would not have been surprised if he never wanted to look at me again. Young-seol, on the other hand, shot me a wicked smile the moment he entered. It was the one he reserved for whenever he thought he'd gotten me into trouble. The jealous little rat loved it when our father scolded me. Yet, Father's face showed no trace of anger. Instead, his eyes held the faded light of a man whose hopes and dreams had been crushed. He'd sacrificed for so long on behalf of a son, who in the end had repaid him with shame and disappointment.

The guilt I felt over my father's sad state was terrible. I was on the verge of giving way to tears, when I noticed something in his hand. What I saw was so disturbing that it sucked the tears back into my eyes and sent a chill running through me. In father's hand was the cleaver that we had used to chop the heads off chickens, back when we still had them. I hadn't seen it in years. Father handed the rusty cleaver to Young-seol and in a mumbled voice told him to wash it in the water bucket and then to sharpen the blade. As my younger brother washed the cleaver, the little troublemaker smirked at me. My entire family now stood in the kitchen around that big, ominous stew pot. A feeling of impending doom crept over me. Had Lee Sung-woo experienced this after his defeat?

My mother, still sobbing, cast her teary gaze up at me. In that instant, my heart raced with hope and uncertainty. Was she going to speak to me, tell me that she forgave me? Then, without a word, she turned her eyes away and looked down at the stew pot. She began to sob even harder.

That was the final straw. I was convinced that they were preparing that pot for me. I had to get out of the house now! Trying not to appear alarmed, I got up and went quietly to my room. No one spoke to me as I slunk away.

In my room I hurriedly packed a few belongings into a small duffel bag and crawled out the bedroom's tiny window. Once outside I was careful not to be seen as I ran to the forest north of our village. The sun had just begun to sink beyond the western end of the valley as I reached the forest's edge. Panicked by the thought of the chicken curse, I ran deeper into the woods. I didn't want anyone from the village to find me as a chicken. I knew that if they did, I'd be cooked for sure.

I was still running when my body suddenly began to shake. The duffel bag dropped from my hand as I lost control of my limbs. Then it happened. With a pop, a bing, and a poof, I found myself buried beneath my clothes. My shirt was like a big sheet that had been thrown over me. Moving out from under it, I

 looked at myself. I was covered with grayish-white feathers. My skinny legs now ended in a pair of four-toed feet. The curse was real. I'd been transformed into a knee-high chicken! When I attempted to speak, all my lip-less beak could manage were pitiful clucking sounds.

As darkness settled over the forest, I grew more and more fearful. There were many foxes in our valley. Even the occasional wolf could be heard howling off in the distant hills. I'd make a tasty meal for any of them should they come across me. I had to hide, but I was reluctant to leave my few belongings. I'd need my clothes in the morning when, or if, I returned to normal. With this in mind, I did my best to conceal them under a pile of loose leaves and branches. I then scurried into the nearest patch of bushes to hide.

For hours I laid unmoving and silent in the underbrush. I waited anxiously for the coming of the dawn, while all about me the growls and hisses of hungry things filled the night. Big things, eager to sink their sharp teeth into a juicy young chicken like myself, were everywhere. I felt more vulnerable in those first few hours than I'd ever felt before in my entire life.

It was some time before the sounds of the predators faded. By then, the moon was high in the sky. The only sounds left in the forest were those of the crickets and the growling of my empty stomach.

I began to entertain the hope that I might actually survive the night.

As the hours of lonely darkness passed in agonizing silence, my hunger grew more and more unbearable. I hadn't eaten since late morning. I was starving. Surrendering to my chicken instincts, I began eating whatever seeds I could find. Then, unconsciously, I started plucking up small insects with my beak and gobbling them down. When I realized what I was doing, I nearly threw up in disgust.

How could I, Kang Goo-shu, champion of the Eastern Village have lowered myself to cowering in bushes and eating filthy bugs? For the first time since I could remember, I cried and cried, until eventually I fell fast asleep.

In the morning I awoke to find myself human once more. I had all ten toes back and the fingers with which to count them. Had last night been a bad dream? If that were true, then what was I doing in the forest? It was then that I noticed

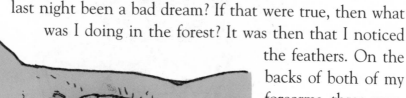

the feathers. On the backs of both of my forearms, three gray-ish-white feathers protruded from my skin.

It was all too real. This was no dream, but rather a cruel nightmare. I nearly screamed in dismay. Was I going to be burdened with chicken parts even during daylight hours? This wouldn't do at all. I'd have to cover my forearms to keep hidden the shame of my awful curse. At the moment, however, I had nothing to use as a wrap. I would have to avoid other people until I'd found some way to hide these conspicuous feathers.

Hurriedly, I put my clothes back on and gathered up my meager belongings. I wanted to get over the northern mountains before the next nightfall. The people of my village would doubtless come after me. I was now the best source of protein on this side of the valley.

As I started off, it dawned on me that once I left the valley, I would likely never return to it again. My family, my friends, my whole world would be left behind for the uncertain future that lay ahead. A life filled with nightly shame, fear and hiding. Shin Young-goo, you foot-funk smelling cheat; this is all your doing!

May 23

I t's been several days since I left my home. I'm now farther from my village than I've ever been and hating every moment of it. The countryside beyond the valley is an endless expanse of mountains and trees. Thick, unfriendly forests cover every speck of the uneven ground. The going has been unspeakably hard. Early on, I feared that people from my village might come looking for me, so I avoided the trails that led out of the valley. It's taken me two days just to get over the outer range of mountains. Now there's no longer a need for me to worry about pursuit. No one from the village would dare come this far out. They, too, would suffer the chicken curse.

Since I didn't have time to pack food before leaving, I've been giving into my chicken nature at night. Slimy bugs and dirty seeds have been all I've eaten for days now. At night I lap up the dew on the leaves with my tiny chicken tongue. It's all very disgusting, but it does the trick. By morning, I'm surprisingly full.

After clearing the mountains I spent another two days stumbling through wild woods. Finally, after circling the same patch of trees for a day and a half, (my rotten eyesight making trouble for me once again), I found an old dirt road that led north. It was barely more than a trail and nearly overgrown with brush, but it offered me the promise of much easier traveling.

May 25

For the last two days the great rivers of heaven have poured down. The sky has been dumping on me nonstop. Rain, rain, rain followed by pails of more wet, cold, soggy, life-sucking, miserable rain. It's bad enough slogging through this downpour during the day when I'm human, but at night, the

cold and wet are absolutely unbearable. Ankle deep mud puddles that I sloshed through as a man become chest high bogs to wade through as a chicken. Also, I've come to learn that wet feathers stink like nothing else in this world — at least nothing still living. The stench and itch of my own mildewing body are threatening to drive me mad.

Last night, after my transformation, I sought shelter in a small, muddy burrow not far from the road. I entered the hole only to discover a young fox already occupying it. My heart froze with fright when I saw the sleeping animal curled up in a ball. Upon my entering its home, the fox immediately awoke and eyed me hungrily. However, after just one whiff of my

stink, it made a horrible hacking sound and ran whimpering past me, abandoning its own lair.

Feeling both relieved and a bit insulted, I cuddled up in the warm spot the fox had left. My rain-soaked belongings were still outside, but I couldn't be bothered with dragging them into the den. I was too exhausted. I immediately fell into a deep sleep, a mistake that I would come to regret.

I awoke in the morning in human form. I found myself naked and crammed between the tight dirt walls of the burrow. My muscular body was too big for the small foxhole. I was stuck. My hands were pinned at my sides with only my head near the burrow's tiny opening. I could breathe and see outside, but was unable to move my arms to free myself. It took me hours to dig myself out of this predicament using only my tongue. Thank the heavens no one was around to witness my humiliation. It's so sad to be me.

May 27

After digging myself out of that fox's burrow the other morning, I retrieved my duffel bag. Everything I owned was thoroughly soaked and my body was covered with mud. The continuing rains soon washed me clean, but I still faced the problem of drying out my clothes. The rains hadn't let up since they'd started and from the gloomy, gray color of the sky, it didn't look like they were about to any time soon. Another few days of this dampness and my clothes would start turning green and grassy with mold.

Returning to the road, I slogged on through the rain and mud until I chanced across a thicket of big leafed trees. Under the cover of their branches, I was able to find some relief from the downpour. I wrung out my clothes and hung them on the branches to dry. Here I sat out the rest of the day cold and restless. Gradually, to my pleasant surprise, the rains finally died down (only after I'd gotten under cover of course). Things soon warmed up again and evening quickly descended over the forest. I passed the night in a comfortable chicken state, my feathers at last drying out.

In the morning, I set out once more heading north. Unfortunately, sometime around mid-morning I misplaced the road. Not paying attention, I'd strayed from it, following instead what I later discovered to be a well-worn animal trail. It was some hours before I realized what a foolish mistake I'd made and by that time, I had already traveled a good distance. Turning around, I tried to retrace my steps and return to the road. But after several hours of fruitless backtracking and aimless circling, I finally gave up. My efforts had only resulted in further confusion.

Disappointed and angry with myself for having made another stupid blunder, I stopped and rested on a large moss-covered rock. Feeling sorry for myself, I took stock of my shortcomings. They seemed to be endless. I had wretched eyesight and apparently my sense of direction was equally worthless. In addition, I was a runaway from my own village and turned into a bug-eating chicken every night. Meanwhile, my arch nemesis, Shin Young-goo, was reaping countless rewards, all thanks to a small mistake I'd made during our fight. Now, to top off this mountainous list of miseries, I found myself lost in these strange woods with sunset only a few hours away.

"What else could conceivably happen to make my life more miserable?" I cried out.

My rhetorical question received an unwanted answer even as the last words left my lips. Within the span of a few breaths, the dreaded rains began anew. This time the downpour was even harder than before. Supernatural forces fired the weighty droplets from the sky like arrows. The merciless heavens had decreed that I, poor Goo-shu, was to undergo yet another trial by water. I was doubly cursed.

Slinging my duffel bag over my shoulder once more, I hopped off the rock and rushed through the woods as quick as I could in search of another dry place to wait out the rains.

Shortly before sunset, my search for shelter was rewarded. Stepping through some light brush, I entered a clearing. In its center stood (and I mean barely stood) an old, abandoned temple. It was

in terrible condition. Vines grew in thick tendrils up its walls and seemed to be the only things keeping it from collapsing in on itself. I

could see that the building's roof had several large holes so I knew the floor wouldn't be completely dry. However, my body was soaked and my teeth were chattering so hard from the cold that I thought they might shatter. So, in spite of the obvious health and safety issues of the place, the crumbling old dump was as good as a palace for now.

I hurried up the slippery stone stairs that led to the entrance and got under what remained of its failing roof. Finding a reasonably dry spot, I dropped my bag. Immediately my nose was assaulted by a smell that went beyond foul. It reeked worse than my father's armpits after he'd spent a hard day working in the fields. It was a rancid odor that burned the nostrils and watered the eyes. It was like dunking my head into a steaming mixture of onion soup and stale vomit. Surely something old and nasty had crawled in here to die.

With daylight fading, I searched about the temple's interior for the poor animal's remains so as to dispose of them. I found nothing. It was soon apparent that age and a serious lack of upkeep were behind the temple's unnaturally potent aroma.

Steeling myself against the smell, I hunkered next to the driest, sturdiest portion of the wall and rested my eyes. Hopefully, the rains would soon pass. I needed to find a better, less odoriferous place to pass the night.

When I opened my eyes again, I was already a chicken. Darkness had fallen over the forest. A bright quarter moon was just starting to creep above the tops of the trees and the rains had slowed to a light sprinkle. I hadn't intended to fall asleep, especially not in this disgusting place. Still, it had kept me dry and my nose seemed to have adjusted to the reek. I only hoped that didn't mean I'd suffered permanent damage to my sense of smell. A thunderous growl from my empty tummy told me the stench hadn't killed my appetite.

Leaving my duffel bag and clothes against the wall, I set out in search of something small and scurrying to eat. Halfway through my bug buffet, I heard noises in the distance. Straining to hear more clearly, I made out two different voices. One belonged to a man and the other to a young girl. They were coming this way.

Panic gripped me. They weren't foxes, but they'd likely welcome a plump chicken for dinner just the same. I rushed to find a place to hide. I remembered seeing a hole in the temple's old wooden floor at the far end of the building. I scurried over to it as quick as my skinny little legs would take me and in I jumped.

I hit the bottom of the hole with a sickening splat. But before I could investigate what it was I'd landed in, I heard the approaching footsteps. The sound of movement upon the creaking floorboards above froze me in place. Not wanting to make even the slightest peep, yet terribly freaked by the icky feeling of what I was standing in, I chanced to look down. The bottom of the hole was a slime pit of gooey, smelly yuck. This explained the deathly stench permeating the temple; it was sitting on a bog of molding barf and I was up to my waist in it. I had to place a wing over my beak to keep from throwing up. The nasty slime was cold and clammy and stuck to my feathers like juicy nose goo. I knew the feathers would disappear in the morning when I turned human. I just prayed that the rank smell would go with them.

It was at this point that I remembered my duffel bag and clothes. I'd left them on the other side of the temple while I searched for food. The intruders would spot my belongings for sure. The bag and clothes were everything I owned in the world. I couldn't let these two interlopers steal them, especially not my silky, pink undershorts. They were imported all the way from China and had been given to me as a birthday present. The shorts were the most valuable of my few possessions and softer than anything in the world, very stretchy too. I rarely wore

my pink shorts for fear of soiling them. I sure didn't want the strangers laying their hands on my undies.

Peeking up from my raunchy hiding place, I saw the man come through the entryway. A young girl roughly my age was right behind him. The man was dirty and dressed in tattered clothes and his head was shaven like that of a monk. At first, I couldn't see the young girl

clearly because she stood in the shadows. When she stepped out into a patch of moonlight, I got my first glimpse of her. She was quite pretty. Her long, black hair was tightly braided into a pair of pigtails. Her clothes appeared only slightly less raggedy than those of the man. In her arms she cradled something. I squinted to bring the fuzzy object into focus. It was an old cloth doll that was falling apart. The doll had on a long, elegant red dress, which appeared to be newer and in far better condition than the doll itself.

It didn't take the intruders long to discover my duffel bag and clothes. The young girl spotted them first. She ran excitedly over to my belongings and called out to the man.

"Look, Father, there are clothes here!" she shouted. "And a bag too."

The man looked about the temple suspiciously to see if the owner (Me!) were present. I ducked my head back into the hole to avoid being seen. When I poked my head up again, the man was on the other

side of the temple standing beside his daughter. Both were busy pawing through my things. I wanted to shout, "Get your filthy beggar hands off my stuff," as they poked through my duffel bag.

When the young girl discovered my pink undershorts, I felt my heart sink.

"Oh, Father, these are beautiful!" the little whelp exclaimed. "I can cut them up and make a coat and matching shoes for my doll."

Upon hearing this, an uncontrollable rage came over me. I squawked furiously in protest and leapt from my hiding place like a chicken possessed. With wings flapping and beak snapping, I charged at the two intruders, intent on protecting my shorts at all costs.

"Father! Look! A chicken!" the girl pointed and shouted.

I was a wing's length away from sinking my beak into the man's foot, when Mr. Bald-Headed-Melon-Face reached down and scooped me up by my neck. I squawked and kicked at the man with my talon-tipped toes, but to no avail. He held me in a firm grip at arm's length. Being restrained in this manner was both undignified and uncomfortable, but I could do nothing to escape.

"This is a plump bird indeed, Daughter. It'll make a fine meal," the man said as he squeezed my neck tighter. "It sure stinks though. We'll have to wash it." The father pinched his nose closed with his free hand.

I was mortified. That stanky, stink, stinker of a stink man had no right to talk. He was a filthy bum. I didn't know what was going to knock me out first, him strangling me or the reek of his rotten breath. Not wanting to find out, I closed my eyes and pretended to pass out. Once I went limp, the man's grip on my neck relaxed and I was able to breathe easier. He then carried me over to the other side of the temple and set me on the ground.

"Start a fire, Daughter," the man said. "I'll tie the chicken up until we're ready to cook it. The meat's always juicier if it's still fresh when it goes on the fire."

The man tied a small string around my neck and fastened it to a wall beam. I then heard him walk away. Once I was certain he wasn't still standing over me, I cracked one eyelid open and took a peek.

The man and his daughter were busy preparing to make a fire. They moved about the temple gathering whatever bits of dry wood they could find and set them in a small pile in the center of the building. Once they'd finished, they squatted over the pile and attempted to light it. Again and again the two tried to start the fire.

"Good luck getting that thing going in this damp slime puddle," I thought to myself. I closed my eyes and relaxed. I wouldn't have to worry about being cooked anytime soon. I had plenty of time to figure out how I was going to escape and get my bag and clothes back.

Suddenly I heard, "Well done, Daughter. That'll be a roaring fire in no time," the man declared in a pleased voice.

Shocked, I opened my eyes wide. There were tiny, glowing embers burning on the pile of debris.

No way! I wanted to cry foul to the heavens for this latest injustice. It wasn't fair. Powerful forces had to be conspiring against me. The old witch's curse never mentioned anything about the chicken boy having to live under a cloud of misfortune the rest of his life.

With the fire started, I knew I had to get away fast. Soon that big, dirty hand would be around my neck again. If that happened, I'd be plucked and cooked for certain.

The man and his daughter were still preoccupied building up the fire, so I went into action. Springing to my feet, I started working on the string around my neck. With an agility that surprised even me, I managed to grasp the knot in the string and began pulling it loose. Even as a chicken I possessed incredible coordination and skill. I had almost freed myself, when suddenly the man turned and noticed what I was doing. He jumped up and rushed to prevent my escape.

"Stop that, you stupid chicken. What are you doing? Stop!" he shouted. The old fool. Who was he calling stupid? He was the one talking to a chicken.

The man reached me just as I pulled the knot loose. Before I could run, his oafish hand was again reaching for my neck. This time I was ready for him. I snapped at the outstretched hand, clamping my sharp beak down hard on one of his fingers. The man bellowed in pain and pulled his hand away, wrenching his finger from my mouth. I was glad he did. That dude's crusty digit tasted awful. The bugs I ate off the ground were cleaner. I tried to spit the taste from my mouth, but it clung tenaciously to my tongue. Still, I took advantage of this chance to escape, running straight for the temple entrance as fast as I could. The girl didn't move to stop me; instead she rushed to her father's side to care for his injured finger.

"Never mind me, get the chicken!" the man shouted as he clutched his finger and stomped up and down in pain.

The father's words came too late, for I was already out the door. In my desperate flight, however, I lost my footing and slipped on the wet floor planks. I tumbled head over heels down the stairs of the temple. With a wet thud, I plopped into a puddle of mud at the bottom. Uninjured, I picked myself up and dashed off into the trees.

Wanting to get as far away as I could, I ran and ran, deep into the

forest. The damp leaves and branches slapped against me. Squinting to

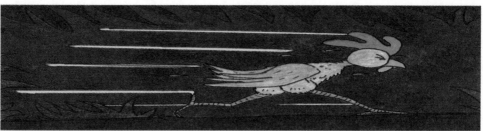

see in the darkness, I strained to pick out a clear path. Straight ahead, I spotted a patch of open sky. There was a clearing in the brush. The twinkling stars danced before me, luring me on. Believing my deliverance to be at hand, I ran forward. The next thing I knew, my face smacked into something hard. Darkness followed.

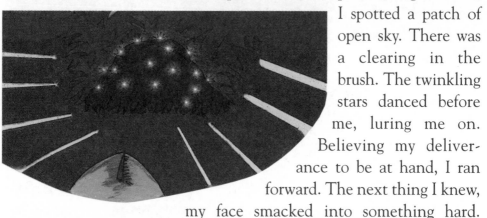

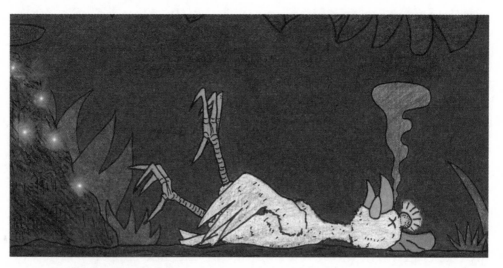

In the morning, I awoke with a headache. Sitting up, I rubbed at my forehead. My hand passed over a large bump and I groaned in pain. The sun was up and I was once again human. I was sitting in the middle of the woods without any clothes. In front of me was a large, black rock, its surface still damp with drops of water that glistened in the morning sunlight. I shook my head in disgust. A lousy wet rock? This was what I'd mistaken for the open sky? The moonlight had made the water on the rock look like stars. I'd run smack into the rock, thinking that it was an opening in the trees. My bottomless stupidity was painfully obvious as I nursed my sore head and bruised ego. This lousy eyesight of mine might prove to be the death of me yet.

Making a wrap for myself out of a few fallen branches, I covered up as best I could and made my way back to the temple. It took only a few minutes to return. Apparently, I hadn't gotten very far before my run in with the rock. If I were lucky, the man and his daughter would still be there and I could retrieve my belongings. I desperately needed my clothes. The leaves were already causing me to itch.

Entering the temple, I found the pair sitting on the damp floor, finishing off a meager breakfast of soaked millet. The young girl's eyes grew large as she noticed me standing in the doorway wearing nothing but a skirt of branches. Picking up on his daughter's sudden change of focus, the father likewise turned and saw me. Shocked at my appearance, the man's jaw dropped open. The grains of soggy millet that he'd been eating fell from his mouth in sticky brown clumps. Hurriedly, he covered his daughter's eyes against the sight of this strange, naked forest weirdo, standing before them.

"Excuse me," I said, as if everything were normal and walked brazenly past them to where my belongings were. Without a word I put my clothes on and checked my duffel bag to make sure everything was still in it. The man and his daughter sat dumbfounded and speechless.

Once I had finished dressing, I turned to face them. After the trouble they'd given me last night, I felt not only compelled but also justified in telling them off. I was about to start yelling but stopped. Looking at them now, in the light of day, I saw something I hadn't noticed last night.

The condition of these two was pitiful. They weren't rotten thieves, just poor and hungry peasants (kind of like me). Last night, the man had appeared large and menacing to my frightened chicken eyes. In actuality, he was a frail, dirty little thing. The deep lines around his eyes and on his weathered forehead told a story of great hardships and worries. My father's face bore such telling lines. Years of struggling to eke out a living in the blighted fields of our village had aged him harshly.

The girl, despite needing a bath almost as badly as I did, was youthful in appearance and as striking as I'd remembered her in the moonlight. She was thin from not having eaten well and her skin was pale. Still, her eyes were large, bright and full of wonder. The doll that she carried was old and tattered. One of its arms was nearly falling off. The long red dress it wore was the only part still in good condition. Made from a finely woven cloth, the dress shimmered like silk. It looked far cleaner than the heavily stained dress that the girl herself wore.

Seeing the father and daughter in this new light, I told myself, here are two people who are having an even tougher go at life than I am, chicken curse not withstanding. How could I begrudge them trying to eat what they believed to be a stray chicken? I'd have done the same. Besides, I couldn't say anything about last night without revealing too much about my own, unique predicament. So, in this instance, no harm, no fowl.

Stepping forward, I introduced myself. "My name is Kang Goo-shu. May I ask your names?"

The man and his daughter rose to their feet. The father was initially hesitant to speak, but then said, "I am Ahn Jung-won and this is my daughter, Ahn Su-jin." The young girl bowed politely and I returned the gesture.

"What brings the two of you way out here?" I asked. In truth, I didn't know where "here" was, but they didn't need to know that.

"My daughter and I are making our way to Kojin fishing village on the eastern coast. I have a cousin there who said he would let me work on his boat. We needed shelter from the storm and happened upon this old temple. The rain has been rough on Su-jin. She tires so easily," said Mr. Ahn, indicating his daughter.

Su-jin held her doll tightly to her chest and stared at me. Her large eyes were fixed on me but not in a creepy or unsettling way. I felt that she was measuring me, judging my character through my words and expressions.

"Her health has not been good of late. We had no money to stay in a village lodge, but by good fortune this old building has sheltered us," Mr. Ahn said.

"It smells bad here, but it's mostly dry," Su-jin said, speaking up.

"Yes, this old place does have a strong air to it, doesn't it?" I said. I looked down at the floorboards and thought about the nasty sludge bath I'd had last night.

Pointing to Su-jin's doll, I commented offhandedly, "That's a pretty dress on your doll, but aren't you a little old to be carrying around a kid's toy?" I asked. After all, the girl was about my age, and I sure wouldn't be caught dead carrying around a doll.

"I don't play with it. I'm not a little kid," Su-jin said defensively. "I just keep it for the memories." Her eyes softened and grew moist.

I wondered. Had I hurt her feelings? Nah! I'm too sensitive to have done that.

"For the memories of her mother," Mr. Ahn said, clarifying his daughter's statement. "My wife made the doll's dress just before she passed away last winter." He wrapped an arm around Su-jin and pulled her gently to him. "The last few seasons were very hard on our village. Most of the crops failed and a lot of people were forced to move away. I lost my land because I could no longer make it produce. Su-jin and I have been traveling ever since."

Their story was tragic but not that uncommon. I could certainly empathize. My village had suffered hardship at seven-year stretches many times over the years. I knew how that could wear people down in both body and spirit.

"I understand," I said. "I come from a

farming village that has endured difficult times as well. I too was forced to leave my home."

"We're sorry for laying claim to your belongings," Mr. Ahn said, pointing to the duffel bag in my hand. "We thought them abandoned. You weren't anywhere about."

"Yes, well, I left them here last night and went…" I paused, trying to think of something to say that would explain why I'd apparently taken off all my clothes to go running naked through the woods. Being unpracticed in the ways of deceit, all I came up with was, "I went in search of food…and…well… I'd once heard an old woman say that moonlight was good for keeping the skin youthful, so I tried to get a moon tan." I'm such a pathetic liar! "I don't think my skin looks any younger though. What do you think?" I said weakly, pretending to look over the backs of my hands.

Mr. Ahn didn't say a word. He didn't have to. The disturbed look on his face said it plainly enough. He thought I was loony. Su-jin's reaction was far more generous. She placed a hand over her mouth to conceal a girlish giggle. She'd found my ridiculous story more funny than off-putting.

It was at this point, that Su-jin noticed the feathers sprouting from the backs of my forearms. Her already large eyes grew wider still with surprise.

"What are those?" she gasped, pointing to the feathers.

Too late, I hurried to cover them with my hands. Before I could, Mr. Ahn saw them too and exclaimed, "My word! Are those feathers?"

This time I didn't bother trying to invent another lame explanation. Shaking my head, I confessed my secret.

"These are my curse." I sighed. I extended my arms so they could better see the feathers. "I was the chicken you tried to eat last night."

Mr. Ahn and Su-jin were speechless. Their eyes blinked in disbelief as they looked from my face to the feathers and back again. They could tell by the seriousness of my tone and my somber expression that I wasn't joking.

It was Su-jin who spoke first. "How could such a thing come to be?" she asked. Her words were full of wonder and amazement. She leaned in closer to look at the feathers.

I decided to answer the question by starting from the beginning, with the origins of the curse. Su-jin and her father listened intently, as I went into my tale of woe. I told them of the witch and the history of our cursed villages. I explained how I had fled my home for fear of being eaten and eventually ended up here. My fantastical story about a curse and chicken boys left them too astonished to speak. Mr. Ahn and Su-jin shook their heads in bewilderment. They'd never heard anything so incredible, but the story couldn't be denied. Here I was, the feathered proof, standing before their eyes.

Finally, Mr. Ahn composed himself enough to speak. "You should cover those up," he said, nervously, pointing to the feathers.

"Yes, Sir, I know, but I have nothing with which to hide them."

Hearing this, Su-jin frowned. "That won't do at all." Tiny wrinkles formed on her forehead and she took on a pondering look. A few seconds later, her youthful face brightened with a broad smile. Pulling the dress off her doll, she proceeded to tear it into two equal strips. When she'd finished, she extended her hand and offered the red fabric to me. "Here, take these and use them to wrap your forearms. Nobody will see the feathers now."

I couldn't believe what this girl was doing for me. Her mother had made that dress. It was her final gift to her daughter. Su-jin was just giving it to me. I'd never been the recipient of such selfless generosity. How could someone who had so little be this willing to share with someone she'd just met? I was put to shame by Su-jin's thoughtful gift and kind spirit. For days now, I had been running around feeling sorry for myself and angry at the world for what had happened to me. There was some justification for me to find fault with my life of late. I was, after all, cursed by powerful magic and I had been forced to flee my home. But the power to twist my heart and fill it with bitterness didn't originate from the curse. It came out of me. Through Su-jin's example, I saw that it didn't have to be so. If this frail, impoverished girl could maintain a strong, generous character in spite of the hardships in her life, then so too could I.

Accepting the wraps, I bowed to Su-jin. "I shall always cherish these: Thank you."

Su-jin smiled and stepped back. My words had brought a blush of pink coloring to her pale cheeks.

Her father put his arm around her shoulders, and hugged her. "I'm very proud of you, Daughter."

I slung my duffel bag over my shoulder. "You have every reason to be, Sir. Few in this world would show such kindness to a stranger. May the remainder of your travels be safe and dry." I bowed to them both, then turned and left the temple. Mr. Ahn and Su-jin followed me to the door.

At the edge of the clearing, I took a last look back. Father and daughter stood at the temple's crumbling entrance waving farewell. I returned the gesture and took one last look at young Ahn Su-jin. I hoped that I would someday see her and her father again.

June 1

The next time I come across other travelers, I really must remember to ask for directions. I left Mr. Ahn and Sujin at the temple without inquiring as to whether or not they knew of any nearby towns. I don't have any money to spend, but in a large town I should be able to find work. I need to wrap my mouth around some real food. All these wild seeds and bugs, while filling, are upsetting to the digestion. The deeper into the woods I go, however, the greater my fear that I might never find my way back to civilization. All the trees, hills, mountains and valleys look so much alike. I've wandered aimlessly for days, uncertain of where I am or where I'm going. The solitude is disheartening and I miss talking with other people. This journal has been the only outlet for my thoughts and feelings.

As I make today's entry, it's just past noon. The sky is clear and the air warm and sweet with the smell of blooming flowers. I've stopped atop a rocky cliff that offers me a great view of the countryside. The shady tree I'm under provides me with a cool place to relax as I write.

I've had this creepy feeling all day. I think I'm being followed. Since before midmorning, I've heard something moving around behind me. Yet, each time I turned around to look, nothing was there. I had hoped that the view from the top of this hill would allow me to spot whomever or whatever was following me. So far I haven't seen anything suspicious. Still, I know I'm not imagining things. Someone or something is definitely out there. I'll remain here another hour or two to verify my hunch. I only hope I don't have bandits on my trail. I've heard scary stories about these wild forests. They're supposed to be filled with thieving criminal types.

June 2

Boy, was I ever right about being followed. The woods are full of much more than just pretty scenery and flowery smells.

This is what happened.

Since I hadn't spotted anyone from atop the hill, I decided to continue on my way. By the time I reached the bottom, the sounds of movement had returned. When I looked back, I still saw no one. I called out, but received no response. Wary, I continued walking. The hours passed, though not in silence. Night grew nearer and the sounds continued. My apprehension grew. Soon I'd be a chicken and at my most vulnerable. I had no idea who or what was out there, but I had to assume the worst. That's what my luck has brought me of late.

Originally, I'd planned to wait out the transformation on one of the nearby hilltops. The threat of being followed changed my mind. Rather than wasting my final moments as a human climbing and tiring myself out, I decided to start looking for a safe place to hide. If there were bandits about, my duffel bag and clothes had to be kept out of sight. I couldn't risk them being stolen. I knew from recent experience that the naked forest kook look didn't suit me.

Moving into a nearby thicket of high bushes, I hunkered down where no one could see as I hid my belongings. More importantly, they wouldn't witness my transformation. Once I stowed my things, I settled in to wait for nightfall.

Minutes later, the dreaded chicken change came over me. With the setting of the sun, my body underwent its horrible transformation. Grayish-white feathers replaced my youthfully perfect skin. An ugly, orange beak sprouted from my handsome face and my arms turned into useless wings. Stepping out from my shoes, I stretched my talon-tipped chicken toes. It was depressing to think that I would spend the remaining nights of my life this way.

The only benefit that I could find in being a flightless, knee-high bird was that I could better escape the notice of would-be bandits.

Using this singular advantage, I pushed my head through the bushes and looked around. Never having seen a bandit before, I was eager to know what one looked like. Were they all as universally ugly as everyone said? Did they wear eye-patches and have hideous scars? I couldn't wait to see.

Long moments passed. The darkening forest remained silent and still. From open patches in the trees above, moonbeams broke through to the forest floor. This gave me more than enough light to spot any bandits out there. I listened for the sound of rustling leaves or snapping twigs, but there was only the chirping of small birds far in the distance. Why was it so darn quiet? Where were my pursuers?

Shortly, my ears picked up the soft, shuffling sound of feet stepping on fallen leaves. The noise was originating from not one source, but several, spread out over a small area. There was definitely more than one person out there and they were trying awfully hard not to be heard. They moved through the brush with deliberate stealth, taking slow, cautious steps. As they got closer, I could make out at least four of them. They outnumbered me, so why hadn't they jumped me during the day? The darkness made it easier for me to hide. They must be stupid bandits.

As I pondered over their strange tactics, I heard a new noise. I still couldn't see the bandits, but I could hear them. It sounded as though they had stopped and were sniffing at the ground.

"What's this about?" I asked myself. What kinds of weirdos sniff the ground? Then I realized; these weren't people on my trail, they were animals. My mind raced, trying to figure out what kind of animals they might be. Foxes didn't hunt together and neither did tigers or bears. That meant...WOLVES!

Panic set in and my skinny chicken legs began to quake. The wolves were only a stone's throw away. These animals hunted by scent and sound, it was no wonder I hadn't seen them. They could keep their distance and track me by my sweet aroma. To them, darkness was an advantage. Hiding in these bushes was now a totally worthless plan. Why? Why? Why couldn't it have been bandits? Big, eye-patch-wearing, stupid, lost in the dark bandits?

I had only one chance and that was to run, and run fast.

I looked around in desperation for an avenue of escape. An opening in the bushes to my rear seemed to be my best shot.

Leaving my bag and clothes behind, I took off. As I scrambled clumsily through the brush, my little legs felt more inadequate than ever. This pathetic feather-covered body wasn't built for either running or fighting. It just tasted good in a soup or with sauce. Why couldn't the witch's curse turn me into a humongous, snarling bear every night? I could be kicking hairy wolf butt right now instead of running to save my own.

Sprinting through the dark, I scurried over stones and fallen logs. I dashed through the underbrush and ducked under low hanging twigs. I was running so hard and so fast that my tongue dangled from my open beak. From behind me there came a horrifying howl. This was followed by the sound of large animals crashing through leaves and branches. My terrified heart leapt within my feathered chest. The wolves had either heard me or smelled me and were giving chase. There was no way I could outrun them. I needed a place to hide: somewhere where the wolves couldn't follow.

Spurred on by their barks and growls, I ran headlong through the forest, looking for a rabbit hole or hollow log. Anything inaccessible to the wolves but large enough to fit my feathered fanny would do. I was way past being picky. Unfortunately, I had moved into a thicker part of the forest. The tree canopy blocked most of the moonlight. I could barely see in front of my face, much less discern a dark hole. What was I to do?

I pushed my way through a thicket of vine-covered brush. Ahead, I spotted a moonlit clearing and a small tree with a gently sloping trunk. Since I hadn't found anything to crawl down and hide in, I'd go up to get away. All I had to do was make it there in one piece.

With renewed hope, I ran towards the tree. I didn't get very far.

In my haste and in the dark, I failed to notice a low branch sticking out from the bush ahead of me. My neck struck it at full steam, knocking me onto my back. Dazed, I stared up at the silhouettes of treetops

and patches of star-filled sky. I gasped for air and coughed painfully, trying to clear my head. I wanted to lie there and rest, to catch my breath, but a loud crash of leaves from directly behind me convinced me otherwise. I was determined not to end up as wolf kibble. Jumping up, I again ran for the tree.

A sudden snarl and the wet snap of powerful jaws near the back of my neck caused my little, pounding heart to skip a beat. I didn't have to look over my shoulder to know that one of the wolves was right behind me. I could feel the beast's hot breath. It barked and wolf spittle hit me on the back of the head.

"This is it," I thought to myself. In another second, the hairy brute would get me.

Panicked and desperate, I ran even faster. I reached the base of the tree and sprinted up it for all I was worth. I was so scared I couldn't breathe, but my legs kept pumping. The sound of wolf claws scratching on tree bark followed me as I scrambled up. I made it to the lowest branch and hopped onto it. I thought I was safe at last when to my sur-

prise a set of powerful jaws snapped down on my tail feathers. The beast pulled me back, trying to get a better bite. I prayed for my tail feathers to come loose, but they didn't. The wolf gave a sharp tug that yanked me off my feet.

My rump was only an instant away from being chomped. Desperate, I flipped onto my back and faced the wolf. I looked straight into its fierce yellow eyes. The beast's wet fangs glistened in the moonlight. The wolf was perched precariously on the trunk of the tree with its head reaching out over the branch. If it pulled me off, I'd be a goner. The other wolves barked and snapped their jaws, anticipating chicken for dinner.

The only weapons at my disposal were the talons on my feet, so I used them. I kicked and scratched at the wolf's nose until it opened its mouth and released me. I scooted back as the startled animal slipped sideways off the tree trunk. The beast crashed onto one of its companions and both wolves yelped in pain and surprise.

For a moment, I lay there on my back, panting. I had made it. I'd survived. I was safe. From the base of the tree, the wolves made no sound. I allowed myself to hope that maybe they'd given up and left.

Regaining my strength, I decided to check. I rolled onto my belly and looked over the edge of the branch. A slobbering wolf muzzle was there to greet me. The furry, frothing, fang-filled face sprang up at me, coming within a hair's breadth of my beak. Letting out a frightened squawk, I pulled back just in time. I got to my feet and moved to the end of the branch where I was certain the wolves couldn't follow should they try climbing the trunk again. My perch wasn't far off the ground, roughly the distance of my human height. Fortunately for me wolves aren't good climbers. Had it been a tiger chas-

ing me, things would've ended very differently. As long as I didn't leave any appendages dangling over the edge, I figured I'd be safe.

For the next few hours, the wolves and I held a stare down. They paced restlessly below me, watching me as I watched them. As the night wore on, I grew tired and eventually dozed off. My sleep was fitful. On several occasions, I nearly rolled off the branch. In each instance, I awoke barely in time to catch myself. The wolves continued to watch me with interest. I only needed to fall once to make them happy, those no life, ear-scratching, butt-sniffing scroungers!

Just before morning, I awoke and checked on the wolves. They were still at the base of the tree, waiting for me to drop into their mouths.

"Ha! Dream on, you filthy, rotten, flea-traps!" I clucked defiantly. Nevertheless, I now realized that sunrise would come long before the wolves' determination ran out. They had to be pretty hungry to be this persistent. It might take another full day of waiting in this tree before their hunger drove them away in search of other prey.

There was no way I would stay stuck in a tree that long. I'd rather meet the wolves head on and take my chances in a fight.

The only good side to the situation was that three of the wolves had already fallen asleep. The fourth mangy cur lay on its stomach, drowsily licking its paws. It wouldn't be long before it dozed off too. Even then, there was no way I'd be able to slip past them undetected. Their hearing was too sharp. When I climbed down the tree, I'd be heading into certain trouble. I knew that I'd need a weapon, if I were going to take on the wolves.

Glancing up at the sky, I saw that I didn't have much time to find one. Sunrise was almost at hand. The transformation would be coming soon, I could sense it in my body.

From my perch, I looked around for something I could use as a weapon – a heavy stone, a sturdy club, or better yet, a big snarling tiger on a leash. Then I spotted a skinny tree with long, straight branches. If I snapped one off, it would make a good staff. All I had to do was to get to the tree before the wolves jumped me. With the dumb animals as zonked as they were, I didn't see that as much of a problem. The element of surprise would be mine. I'd hit the ground running and reach

the tree before the wolves had figured out that the chicken they were waiting for was now a mighty fighter who aimed to beat their hairy bottoms.

Suddenly, I received an unexpected surprise of my own. My transformation back to human started sooner than expected. The surge of the change rushed upon me. My body began to tremble. Then with a pop, a bing and a poof, I turned human again. I was now sitting naked on a branch that was too small to support my new weight. With a loud crack, the branch snapped and I fell, landing on two of the resting wolves. They yelped sharply and then were silent. My fall had knocked

them out. Unfortunately, the commotion had awoken the remaining wolves. They sprung to their paws and snarled at me with bared teeth. Their yellow eyes were like angry slits focused on my throat.

Without a second to waste, I jumped to my feet and made a bee-line for the tree that I'd spotted. The wolves took off after me. I reached the tree with the nasty animals hot on my bare butt. Grabbing the nearest branch, I snapped it free of the trunk. I then circled around the skinny tree just as the wolves hurled themselves at me. Both missed, but quickly spun about to come at me again. I stood with the scrawny tree between the wolves and myself. I'd let the wolves make the next move. I didn't have to wait long.

One of the wolves began circling to my left. I kept my eyes on the beast but didn't turn to face it. I allowed it to take my flank and to think me vulnerable. Believing it had the edge, the wolf rushed at me. With lightning fast reflexes, I swung my makeshift staff around and caught the animal in the side of the head. The power of this mighty blow knocked the beast to the ground where it lay unconscious in a tangle of vines.

That was one down and one to go.

I hoped that the last wolf would be intimidated and run away. Even a dumb animal should know when it's facing a superior opponent. Regrettably, the wolf decided to make things difficult for itself.

The angry beast barked and growled as if to build up its courage. Then, when it felt ready, it charged. Immediately, its snapping muzzle was introduced to the pointy end of my staff. The wolf let out a pained yelp before it passed out from the blow.

I looked around to be sure that the other wolves were still unconscious. Seeing that they were, I hurried off with staff in hand to retrieve my clothes. I was afraid that more wolves might be in the area, or, even worse tigers or bears. I wasn't going to stick around and find out. I'd had enough of nature for a while. The sooner I found a town or village, the better I'd like it.

Returning to where I'd left my clothes and duffel bag, I got dressed on the double and headed off in search of civilization. I kept the staff with me for continued protection. It wasn't only when I took the form of a chicken that I needed to worry. The forest was not a safe place. It was full of predators, both of the four-legged and the two-legged variety.

On a dramatic whim I decided to name my new weapon, believing that weapons with names always sound cooler. I soon settled on Wolf Whacker. The name seemed appropriate considering how I'd first used the staff. Later, I would need to clear away the little branches from it to make it into a proper weapon.

I remained on edge all throughout the morning. My hands never once loosened their grip on Wolf Whacker. I would raise it defensively whenever I heard the sound of leaves rustling. Thankfully, my trek through the woods went without further incident.

Just after mid-day, I came across a well-traveled dirt road. It was wide and bore the signs of recent use. There were numerous deep tracks in the road, indicating that it was often used by heavy wagons.

I was elated. Finally, I was free of the woods and would soon encounter other people.

The road ran east and west for as far as I could see. Faced with having to choose a direction, I decided on east. Su-jin and her father may have taken this road on their way to the Eastern Sea. If I were fortunate, I might see them again. I'd welcome the sight of their friendly faces. Besides that, I'd never seen the sea, or any body of water larger than a pond. I was curious as to what so much water might look like.

A short time later, I had my second piece of good fortune for the day. This time it came in the form of a pair of traveling entertainers. Had it not been for the armbands Su-jin had given me, I would've been nervous to stop and talk with them. But with the feathers on my arms well covered, I eagerly approached and greeted the two men. The entertainers were friendly and helpful. They told me of a town that they'd just come from, only a few hours farther down the road. They said I could easily make it there before dark.

I was glad for the news and looked forward to seeing the town. It would be a real treat for me. The Eastern and Western Villages of my valley were the only two communities I'd ever known and they were both tiny.

After warning the travelers to be wary of wolves, we said our farewells and parted. I hurried on my way, anxious to reach the town before nightfall. My mind raced in anticipation. I couldn't imagine what wonders the place might hold. Surely there would be many travelers such as myself and shops and traders and foods of all kinds. My tummy growled just thinking about all the lip-smacking yummies that a town would have to offer.

June 4

Yesterday, I was forced to postpone my visit to the town and instead had to do a bit of hiding. A large troop of Koguryo soldiers was passing through the town just as I arrived on its outskirts. I'd heard stories that soldiers forcibly took young men from their villages to serve in the army. That was not the life for me. I wasn't going to end up as some spear-toting toady serving a far off king for whom I didn't care a wit. So, as the soldiers went by, I concealed myself off to the side of the road and watched.

The line of troops seemed to go on for hours. Hundreds of men and dozens of horses and wagons moved by in slow procession. I'd seen soldiers in the past. Some years ago, a small group on horseback had camped at the edge of our valley. From a distance, my friends and I had watched them. They had nice uniforms and polished metal armor with cool looking plumes in their helmets. In contrast to those men, these guys were a scruffy and unenthusiastic lot. Many wore sloppy, mismatched uniforms and practically no armor. Their movements told me that they were weary and sick. There wasn't a smiling face among them. Even the officers on horseback looked glum. I wondered if they'd just come from a battle. I felt sorry for them.

As I waited for this procession of the miserable to pass, I made use

of the time by clearing away the tiny branches from my staff. It wasn't long before Wolf Whacker was splinter-free.

After the last of the soldiers and supply wagons was out of sight, I came out of hiding. The way was finally clear for me to proceed, but now sunset was fast approaching. I decided to play it safe and wait until morning to go into town. Assuming there were no wolves around, I'd be safer hiding in the woods outside of town than I would be wandering the streets as a chicken.

For a pleasant change, nothing terrifying happened to me that night. I ate what bugs and seeds I could find and then watched the town folk from the shadows of the forest. I was impressed by the size of the place. It was many times larger than my tiny village. Some of the buildings were even two stories tall. I desperately wanted to walk along the streets. I could only imag- ine the wondrous varieties of food that the town's marketplace would have to offer. The thought made my beak water.

That night I had to content myself with just looking in from the outside. From the tree line, I savored the smell of real food cooking in nearby homes. Falling asleep, I passed the hours until dawn with dreams of tasty foods and new sights.

The bustle of activity began early the next morning. City folk didn't rise quite as early as farmers did, but they were up and about their business before I had made my transformation back to human.

Eager to begin sightseeing, I quickly got dressed. I paid particu- lar attention to my arm wraps, making sure they were on secure. Even a casual glimpse of the feathers on my forearms would bring me unwanted attention.

The town's broad streets were more than twice as wide as those of my village. They were also quite a bit dirtier. I was disappointed to see how much filth there was on the ground. There were heaps of fly-covered animal poop everywhere. The town's folk surely didn't let their animals take dumps wherever they pleased. In my village, the animals were penned. They weren't allowed to poop in front of our houses. The caravans of merchants that passed through with their oxen and horses had to be to blame. The people that lived in town would never soil the ground in front of their own homes or businesses like that.

Keeping a close watch on where I stepped, I strolled about the town. I found the newness and size of the place overwhelming. The houses along the streets were large and pleasing in appearance. Most had colorful tile roofs and painted walls. None of them were made of ugly mud bricks and old thatch as were those of my village.

The clothes that the people wore were of great fascination to me. They were even more colorful than the walls and roofs of the buildings. I saw some styles that were known to me and many others that were not. Every face was new and unfamiliar. Back in my valley, I was acquainted with everyone living in the two villages; here, everyone was a stranger. There were perplexing foreign languages to listen to and unusual dialects to struggle to understand. The world suddenly seemed so much bigger than it had been. Leaving my valley wasn't such a bad thing after all if it allowed me to see all these wondrous sights. The town's splendor did have one drawback. It made me feel like the poor country cousin. In contrast to those around me, my appearance was dismal. My clothes needed washing badly and my body smelled every bit as awful as I looked. I didn't fit in with these sophisticated people. That isn't to say that I was made to feel unwelcome. No one gawked at me or laughed. In fact, I was paid no attention at all. The town's folk must have been used to seeing grungy strangers like me.

I walked up and down every street at least a half dozen times. The place was so busy with the comings and goings of traders, travelers and shopkeepers that even the same street seemed new and unexplored by the time I returned to it later.

Finding my way back to the town's main market-street, I walked slowly past the various shops and table displays. On one table were pottery items from all over Korea and China. On another, bolts of bright cloth were piled as high as my head. I looked at one bolt of fine, pink cloth and smiled, thinking of my silky, pink underwear.

The delicious smells coming from nearby restaurants were a constant distraction. I stopped to look in each door to see what people were eating. The smells of different kinds of kimch'i, frying noodles, millet soup, cooking fish and roasting strips of spicy pork were positively maddening. I wished that I had some money. I could've spent a week and a small fortune just eating. Thinking about money reminded me that I needed to find work. I didn't believe I'd have any trouble in this regard. A town this size would have plenty of opportunities for a strong, industrious, young man such as myself. With a good job, I could afford to eat well.

Food was all I could think about as I walked past stall after stall of meats and produce. As I passed the stalls, vendors called out to me, offering me bargains on whatever it was they were selling. Looking at all the food on display, I grew even more ravenous with hunger. That is until I came to a stall selling uncooked chickens. The decapitated birds hung upside down from an overhead rack. The sight caused my appetite to leave immediately. My enthusiasm for town life waned as I pondered the consequences. Staying in a place like this would definitely be exciting, but it came with its own danger. With so many people around, I risked being discovered for what I am, a chicken boy. I didn't want to end up the same as those headless chickens, hanging upside down in the market. Whatever job I took would have to be strictly day work.

It was at this point that I heard a young voice cry out from around a corner up ahead. Curious, I went to investigate.

Following the voice, I turned down a narrow alley which opened into a small courtyard. At the far end of the courtyard were four boys, roughly my age. They were standing over a much younger boy, who was lying on the ground. Just behind the young boy was a cart of fresh vegetables tilted onto its side. One of the cart's wheels had been smashed and most of the vegetables it carried had spilled out, littering the ground.

I stood at the corner of the alley, unnoticed by the boys in the courtyard, and listened as the largest of them spoke.

"You tell your father, he don't want his carts to go without wheels, he pay us by tomorrow," the large boy said to the little one. For added emphasis, one of the other boys gave the little guy a swift kick in the chest.

That was all I had to see to know what was going on here. The four large boys were bullies and what's more, extortionists. I may have been trained specifically to defeat my opponent from the Western Village, but I'd also been taught to fight for what was right. Four older boys beating up on one little one to get money was definitely not right. I determined right then and there to put a stop to it.

Stepping into the courtyard where the bullies could see me, I cleared my throat loudly. The four bullies looked up. The largest of them, whom I assumed to be the leader, took notice of my filthy appearance.

In a rough voice he said, "What you want, Dirt Boy?"

"What I want is for you and those three head-scratching monkeys next to you to keep your nose-picking hands off that kid."

"Is that so?" the lead bully laughed.

"It's so. And after I'm finished with you, you're going to fix that cart." I pointed with Wolf Whacker to the damaged cart.

The bullies laughed at me. "You got big plans for a squinty-eyed stranger," one of them said.

"Yeah, squinty," chuckled the shortest of the four bullies. From his clownish demeanor and parrot-like speech, he obviously wasn't the intellectual of the group. Once I beat the others, he'd fold without a fight.

"If you four are as stupid as you appear, then this should be a really quick fight," I said, dropping my duffel bag to show that I was ready to rumble.

"Fight?" the lead bully scoffed. "If you got any money, I be happy take it from you after I step on your face. But there not gonna be no fight, Dirt Boy."

"Look at him, standing there squinting at us. He's like an old man that can't find his own nose," piped in another of the bullies.

"Yeah, nose. Old guy," laughed the short bully.

In a bored voice I replied, "If you're all done flapping those soon-to-be fat lips of yours, I'd like to commence thrashing you."

"Fine, Stink Boy. You wants a thrashing, then you gonna get one. Woo-chang," shouted the lead bully, addressing the boy that had made the comment about my squinting. "Go pound him flat like a rice cake," he ordered.

Woo-chang wasted no time on subtlety. He rushed forward with one hand outstretched to grab me and the other chambered back ready to throw a punch.

I sidestepped his reckless charge and elbowed the bully in the nose. Woo-chang dropped to his knees and clutched at his nose, whimpering like a little girl.

"Unlike me, I don't suppose you'll have any difficulty locating your nose now, will you?" I said to the bully. I wanted to make his friends as angry as I could before they attacked. An angry opponent is often clumsy and always one-dimensional. He'll attack with no thought of defense or consideration for strategy and is easy to anticipate and counter.

The lead bully's face grew red with rage. Turning to the boy next to him, he shouted, "Go get him!" He pushed the boy towards me. "Beat him like a ratty, mutt dog in the street."

This bully was less brazen than the first. He approached more cautiously. Keeping his hands raised, he circled in on me. I stood my ground, holding Wolf Whacker down at my side to appear less threatening. I wanted to lure him in closer. Once the bully was near enough, he lunged at me with fists flying.

I easily ducked and dodged these sloppy blows without even having to raise my hands in defense. The bully followed up his punches with front and sidekicks aimed at my stomach. Those, too, I avoided effortlessly. I let the clumsy clod continue to throw more punches and kicks at me until he began to get frustrated and tired. Once I saw his arms lower slightly, I moved on him. The bully jabbed defensively, but I ducked the punch and shot in from below with a palm strike that caught the creep under his chin. The bully's head rocked back. He staggered a few steps, wobbled, then finally his knees gave out and he dropped to the ground like a wet rag.

Addressing the lead bully, I faked a yawn and said, "I'm getting bored playing with your younger sisters. Are you ready to step out for your turn at a beating?"

"You ain't be bored no more, Dirt Boy. Now I pound you myself," the ill-spoken wretch growled. He raised his hands and lumbered towards me. He was a whole head taller than I was and much heavier. He figured to use his greater size to his advan-tage by rushing me.

Not the least bit intimidated, I stood my ground. Just before the bully reached me, I raised Wolf Whacker and thrust its point straight out. The dumb thug ran his nose right into it. Shouting and cursing in pain, he stepped back

and clutched at his nose. Immediately, I followed up with a finishing move. I dropped and spun on one knee, delivering a drop sweep to the bully's ankles. I caught both his legs squarely, knocking his feet out from under him. The bully's bubbly, fat butt hit the ground with a loud thump.

Jumping to my feet, I cast a hard look at the remaining bully. The short one, who had repeated everything his friends said, sniveled and fell to his knees.

The spineless coward rubbed his palms together and pleaded, "Not me too. Don't hit me. I'm be a good person from now on, I promise," he whimpered.

"Can I trust you on that?"

"Yes, yes. You can trust me," he said earnestly.

"What's your name?" I asked him.

"Kim Ju-sung," he replied nervously.

"Well, Kim Ju-sung, I want you to go get the supplies needed to repair that wheel," I said, pointing to the damaged cart.

The bully nodded. "Right away," he said, and took off.

The other bullies were still on the ground. They nursed their bruises and looked up at me fearfully. None of them dared rise just yet, afraid that I'd give them another well deserved trouncing. Ignoring them for the moment, I went over to the young boy that they'd been terrorizing and knelt down beside him. As I offered him a hand up, he stared at me wide-eyed and full of amazement. I helped dust the dirt off of him and introduced myself.

"I'm Kang Goo-shu, and you are?"

"Jung Myoung-won," the boy responded brightly.

"You're all right?"

"Yes, Sir."

"Good," I then turned back to address the bullies. "When your friend gets back with the supplies, you'll all help to fix the cart. Clear?" I gave their leader an especially hard look.

All three bullies nodded.

I signaled for them to get up. "You're also going to stop bothering this boy and his family. If you don't, I promise, you'll be seeing me and my squinty eyes again."

"Yes, of course," the three replied nervously as they rose to their feet.

Confident that they would do as instructed, I returned to Myoung-won.

"You're sure you're not hurt?"

The boy was quick to answer. "Yes, Sir, I am fine thanks to you. My father will be so happy to hear about what you have done for my family and me. Please let me take you to him. He will want to thank you himself."

I agreed to follow the boy, but before leaving stopped to give the bullies some final instructions.

"Don't steal any of the vegetables. Just load them back onto the cart after you're done fixing it and deliver it to the Jungs."

"Yes, Sir," the lead bully said softly, keeping his head lowered.

Myoung-won led me out of the alley and around the corner. Crossing the main market street, he took me to his family's business. By the mercy of the Great Buddha, it was a restaurant. This was the first time I'd ever been in one. It was spacious. The seating area alone was larger than my entire house. It had a lightly lacquered wood floor and beautiful scrolls hung from the walls. There were numerous large and small wooden tables but not a single customer. It appeared that the place hadn't opened for business. It was still too early for most people to eat lunch. However, I was more than ready to scarf down; if only I'd had some money. The wonderful smells coming from the kitchen were making my mouth water. It brought back memories of the delicious meals that my mother had prepared. She was such a good cook. I missed sitting down to dinner with her and the rest of my family.

I was just beginning to feel homesick when Myoung-won began shouting. "Father, Mother," he yelled as we stood in the doorway.

A middle-aged man and woman rushed from the kitchen. Both were short and chubby. Obviously, they enjoyed their own cooking. This was a good indicator that the food was top-notch. When the Jungs saw me, they stopped in their tracks and stared. I imagined that they didn't know what to make of my filthy appearance. Confused, the couple looked to their son for an explanation.

"He saved me, Father. He stopped the bullies from beating me up and he's making them fix our vegetable cart," Myoung-won said in a rush.

This hastily offered explanation did little to clear up things. Still puzzled, the Jungs urged their son to calm down and start from the beginning.

Myoung-won took a deep breath and proceeded to tell his parents about how the bullies had set upon him in the alley, shoving him around and breaking a wheel on the cart. The thugs had wanted to force the Jung family into paying protection money. If the family didn't pay, the bullies threatened to trash the restaurant. With enthusiastic detail, Myoung-won told his parents how I'd miraculously showed up and rescued him. His retelling of the fight was especially animated. It went so far as to include exaggerated sound effects and mock punches and kicks.

When they'd heard the whole story, the Jungs invited me to sit and rest. They were bubbling over with gratitude for what I'd done for them and their son. Apparently, the bullies had been bothering shop owners on this street for months. They would break things and scare away the customers of any businesses that didn't pay them money each week. Mr. Jung said that since the bullies had been so soundly beaten, the other local shop owners wouldn't be afraid to stand up to them in the future. I'd done the entire community a great service. Mrs. Jung went so far as to call me a hero, a title I didn't think I deserved. In appreciation, she offered to fix me any meal I wanted.

Thrilled by the offer, I asked for a large bowl of mon-doo soup. My mother was exceptionally good at making the small, meat filled dumplings.

Smiling, Mrs. Jung said she'd cook them right up. She also suggested that while I waited I might like a nice bath. I got the impression that as grateful as she was, she didn't feel comfortable with me sitting in her clean restaurant in my filthy state.

Not wanting to pass up a choice opportunity, I graciously accepted her generous offer.

While Mr. and Mrs. Jung went into the kitchen to prepare the meal, Myoung-won took me into the small central courtyard of their house, located just behind the restaurant. He prepared a hot bath for me, warming the water with stones that had been heated in a fire. I was careful to leave my arm wraps on as I got into the bath. Myoung-won thought this rather odd and asked me why I didn't remove them. I casually brushed the question aside and being a polite boy, Myoung-won let the matter drop.

My bath was like a slice of heaven after the hellish sufferings I'd endured over the last few weeks. Every once in awhile, Myoung-won would come along and replace the cooled stones in the tub with hot ones, fresh from the fire. In this way, I was kept in toasty warm ecstasy for the duration of my long bath. As I was soaking, Myoung-won was kind enough to wash my clothes and then hang them out to dry.

After I had finished bathing, Myoung-won lent me some of his father's clothes to wear while mine dried. I was then led back to the

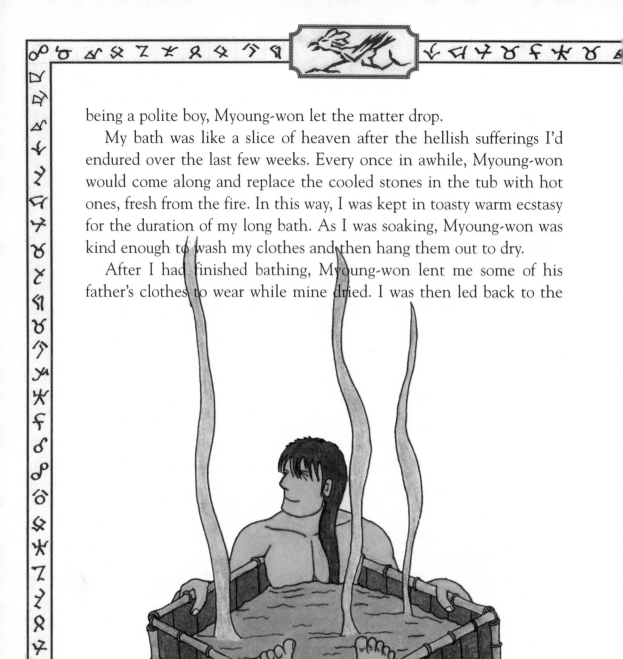

restaurant. The meal that his parents had prepared for me was already laid out on one of the large tables. By this time, the restaurant was open. Several customers were sitting at other tables, waiting for their meals. Mr. Jung joined me at the table while Mrs. Jung and Myoung-won returned to the kitchen to ready the other customers' orders.

Together, Mr. Jung and I dined on delicious mon-doo soup with diced bamboo shoots, kimch'i, juicy strips of beef dipped in salted sesame seed oil and a host of vegetable side dishes. The food was so good that I gorged myself like a pig. I was going to be one stuffed chicken tonight. I hoped I wouldn't have to outrun any predators.

After finishing off every succulent morsel of food on the table (as well as a few that accidentally fell under it), Mr. Jung and I got to talking. I was anxious to hear news about the town and the country in general. Being a naturally gabby fellow, Mr. Jung was more than willing to share with me everything he'd heard from his friends and customers.

As our conversation progressed, I learned much about the happenings outside of my tiny valley. The kingdom of Koguryo was in turmoil. Our old king, King Gogook-yang, had died just last month. His seventeen-year-old son, Tam-duk, had assumed the throne. The new king's first order of business was to change his name to Young-lak. King Young-lak was currently busy fending off attacks from the Chinese state of Huyeun to the northwest. At the same time, he's also battling with the kingdom of Paeckhe to the southwest and skirmishing with Shilla forces along the southern border. No wonder the troops I'd seen the day before looked so tired. The country was rife with conflict. This wasn't anything new, however. Our kingdom was always fighting someone over something. Mr. Jung explained the latest reasons for the conflicts, but I just couldn't understand any of it; so many people killing one another like that. It made no sense. Why couldn't they just choose champions and have it out, one on one? That's how we did it back in the valley. I had to admit that in retrospect, our system hadn't turned out well for me. But at least we weren't running around killing, burning and pillaging.

Leaving the depressing topics of war and politics, Mr. Jung spoke of more local concerns. He warned me to avoid traveling through the mountains to the north. A particularly rough band of bandits had set up operations there. They exacted a steep "toll," as they liked to call it, from any travelers passing through the mountains.

It was at about this time that the four bullies arrived with the newly repaired cart of vegetables. Under my stern watch, they unloaded the veggies and apologized to the Jungs for their misbehavior.

Satisfied with the bullies' contrition, I let them go, but not before warning them against a return to their unruly ways. When they'd gone, Mr. Jung and I returned to our conversation.

My host and I continued talking for another hour or so. Most of the topics he brought up were, quite frankly boring. Local political scandals and the growing cost of fresh produce were of little interest to me, but I pretended to listen anyway. All the while I was trying to think of a way to ask him about a job, if not in his restaurant, then in some other establishment. Then Mr. Jung happened to mention an odd story that he'd overheard a customer telling to some friends a few months earlier.

The man had been on his way to visit relatives in another town south of here. It was nearing sunset and the light was beginning to fade. The man pressed on, determined to get to his relative's home that same day. While making his way over a hill, he chanced to notice a strange glimmer of light out of the corner of his eye. Focusing in that direction, he saw the hazy image of a great tower on a distant hilltop. It was shimmering in the fading sunlight. The man stared at it for a moment, then, inexplicably, the mysterious tower disappeared, evaporating like the morning mist.

Mr. Jung said that, had he not heard two very similar accounts from other travelers years earlier, he'd have thought the man was touched in the head. As it was, Mr. Jung was convinced that there was something magical in the hills to the south. It was something unnatural and it frightened him.

This story about a disappearing tower didn't scare me. In fact, I was intrigued. My chicken curse originated from magic. If this mysterious tower were magical too, then perhaps something or someone there could offer me a cure. It was certainly worth investigating. I decided to seek out the tower. If it held a solution to my curse, I was determined to have it.

Forgetting all about asking for a job, I instead pressed Mr. Jung for more information on the tower. He was more than happy to tell me the two other stories that he'd heard. After Mr. Jung had finished recounting the tales, I felt I had at least a general idea of where to start my search. I determined that the tower lay somewhere in the mountains and hills not far to the south. The tower, it seemed, only appeared for brief moments during sunset and sunrise.

Although the information I'd gleaned from the stories wasn't very specific, it was sufficient to begin a search for the tower and I was eager to set off. Once my clothes were dry, I thanked the Jungs for their hospitality. Between the excellent meal they'd provided me and the information about the tower, I felt that I'd been overcompensated. The assistance I'd given them had been minor. In return, they were sending me off with a stuffed belly and a heart full of hope. When Mrs. Jung offered me several dumplings and some cooked millet wrapped in paper to take with me, I felt guilty. I was, however, in no position to turn down such tasty gifts. I accepted them with deep thanks and a courteous bow. Bidding the Jungs a fond farewell, I set out late that afternoon to look for the tower.

June 6

I reached the area where the eyewitnesses had seen the tower. Climbing to the top of a low mountain that overlooked most of the surrounding countryside, I waited for sunset. If my suspicion about the tower only appearing during sunset and sunrise were correct, I'd only have a short time in which to spot it before it vanished again. Another concern I had was my transformation. It would take place at the exact same time. Spotting the tower while my body was in the midst of shifting form wouldn't be easy. Still, I was determined to find it.

Scanning the valleys and hills, I kept a close look out for likely spots where a giant tower might appear. The sun was just beginning to sink below the horizon. If a mystical tower were out there, it should be appearing at any moment. My eyes darted back and forth, scrutinizing each and every hilltop. Before I could give the entire area a thorough looking over, my transformation started. By the time I crawled out from under my clothes, the sun had already set. Disappointed, but not despondent, I vowed to be ready again in the morning. I'd find that tower. I just knew I would, if it existed.

The next morning at sunrise I looked in every direction, but saw no sign of the tower. I decided to move to a new location on the mountain, one that offered a different angle of the terrain. The whole region was riddled with tiny hills, low mountains and gorges. I knew it might take days to see it all, but I had the time.

June 11

The next night and the following morning played out the same. I looked. I saw nothing. I transformed. Once more I decided to move to a different peak of the mountain. I was beginning to fear that the tower might not exist at all. I was sure Mr. Jung hadn't been pulling my leg with his stories about a magical tower. He had no reason to do such a rotten thing. However, those supposed eyewitnesses were another matter. They might just have been a bunch of jokers telling tall tales. I tried hard to convince myself that wasn't the case. The tower did exist. It had to and I would find it. Inside it there would be a magic spell to rid me of these darn chicken transformations. Yeah, right! Who was I kidding? How could such a tower really exist? I was probably wasting my time, but heck, what else did I have to do?

I passed the third evening perched atop a rocky outcropping that jutted from the backside of the mountain. As the sun began to rise, I could feel the transformation to human beginning. Frantically, I searched for some sign of the tower before the change totally distracted me. Then, out of the corner of my eye, I spotted a shimmer. I turned to look. At first, I thought it only a patch of morning mist. I squinted hard

to focus better and saw the outline of a tall, dark shape resting atop a distant hill. For the briefest instant, the image of a gray stone tower became perfectly visible. In the span of a few breaths, it faded away, like mist in sunlight.

My patience had paid off. I'd found the tower.

I rushed to put on my clothes. The hill where I'd seen the tower was quite far. Before the tower had vanished, I'd made careful note of its position. A large portion of the hill's southern slope was bare rock. It would be easy to identify. I would have to hurry, if I wanted to get there before nightfall.

It took me nearly the entire day to reach the hill where the tower had appeared. Many of the surrounding hills looked so much alike. It was difficult to distinguish one from another, especially with my undependable eyesight. It wasn't until I arrived at the base of the rock slope, that I had seen from the mountaintop, that I knew I was in the right place. Climbing the steep hill, I trekked through the dark woods that covered much of the hillside. At last I came to a large clearing. The area was completely empty with no sign of a tower anywhere. I walked into the middle of the clearing and looked back towards the mountain and the rocky outcropping where I'd stood at dawn. This was the right spot, only minus the tower.

As I looked around for anything of a mystical nature, I noticed the deathly silence. All morning the woods had been full of sounds. The squeaks and chirps of living things going about the business of life had filled the air. Here in this clearing, however, there was nothing, only an eerie calm. Even the wind was gone. Looking up in the sky and in the trees, I didn't see a single bird. The scampering little squirrels that were so plentiful in the forest below were also noticeably absent. The quiet of the place was creepy. Did the animals know something I didn't? I explored the entire clearing, but aside from the unbroken stillness found nothing out of the ordinary. There was no sign that a huge tower had ever been here.

It was late in the afternoon and I was tired. My feet needed a rest. I'd been moving at a fast pace since morning. I leaned back against the trunk of a tree and finished off the last of the dumplings that Mrs. Jung had given me. Chewing on the doughy bread, I wondered how it was possible that something as large as a tower could appear and then, moments later, vanish away to nothing? Was what I saw that morning an illusion, or merely a trick of light? Or perhaps, it sprung up from beneath the ground? I'd know soon enough. It wouldn't be long until sunset and the tower's next appearance.

As the sun's light faded, I stood and watched the clearing with undivided attention. Once the tower appeared I would run to it and get inside as quickly as possible before it could disappear. I'd be along for the ride the next time it vanished.

As the sun dipped behind the farthest of the western mountains, the tower began to materialize. At first it was just a quivering shimmer of light, so faint as to be unnoticeable unless one were looking straight at it. Then gradually, a massive, gray object began to form. Within seconds, the undefined shape took full substance and a gigantic stone tower became fully visible. The enormous structure looked as real and

as solid now as if it had always been there.

With my duffel bag and staff in hand, I ran as fast as I could towards the tower. I'd gotten only a few steps when suddenly I felt my body strike something. There was nothing there that I could see, but I had definitely run into something. It felt like a wall, as if the very air itself had become thicker, denser. Whatever the invisible barrier was, it reacted to my effort to pass through it. All around me the air appeared to ripple outwards as if I were a tossed stone disturbing the calm surface of a pond. I pushed through the barrier with difficulty. Once on the other side, I stopped and looked back. Everything appeared normal. There was no evidence of a barrier.

Having no time to waste pondering the phenomenon, I hurried towards the tower. I managed only a few steps before being halted. This time it was the chicken transformation that stopped me. I was only paces shy of reaching the tower's gray stone walls when the change began. My hands and arms turned into wings and the duffel bag and staff, I was carrying, dropped to the ground. My clothes enveloped my shrinking body, making it impossible for me to see. I was again a chicken. What a bummer!

Shuffling out from under my shirt and pants, I shook my feathered head and looked up. I was relieved to see that the gigantic structure was still there. Looking around, I saw that the forest, mountains and sky remained unchanged. The tower obviously hadn't sunk beneath the ground. This eliminated one theory I had developed to explain its disappearance. I could conclude from my familiar surroundings that I hadn't been spirited away to some far off magical land either. So what had happened? Perhaps the invisible barrier I'd passed through had something to do with it? Was it an otherworldly doorway? I suspected that to anyone standing outside the barrier, it would seem as if the tower had disappeared and I along with it. From this side, everything was as it had been; only now there was a giant stone tower.

I shook my head in confusion. This stuff was way beyond me. I was no sorcerer. All I knew for certain was that there was magic at work here. Who could be behind it? Was it the work of gods or perhaps demons? Whoever they were, I was sure they'd know how to remove my curse. I just hoped that they would be willing to help. Anybody powerful enough to create a huge, disappearing tower could easily turn me into a chicken full time or something even worse. I'd have to be careful. But first, I needed to find a way into the tower.

I stepped back a few paces to view the structure in its entirety. I marveled at how it seemed to go up forever. I knew that being reduced to one fourth of my normal size exaggerated my perceptions. The tower couldn't really be that tall. However, from a chicken's standpoint, it was still really big. I tried making out some of the structure's details. The tower was cylindrical in shape. Each of its levels was marked by a set of decorative tile eaves. These made the tower resemble a giant pagoda. The tiles came in a variety of different colors. On one level they were a deep umber and red, while those of another were teal blue and dark purple. A third level's tiles were orange and bluish gray. It was all very colorful. Stone figurines rimmed the edges of the eaves. Each figurine was carved in the likeness of a different animal. My poor eyes could only make out a few of the animals represented. The carvings of a horse, pig and dog were the clearest to me.

From where I stood, I counted at least seven stories. The two uppermost levels had oddly shaped windows that resembled sinister eyes. I didn't see any lights coming from them, but they looked like they might be large enough for me to enter. It would be a hard climb to reach the windows. The blocks making up the tower wall were large and the spaces between them suitable for use as hand or footholds almost impossibly small. Climbing would be my backup plan in case I failed to find a better means of entering the tower before morning. For now I'd focus on a more practical way in, something that a puny chicken like myself could use.

I decided that a bit of exploration was in order. Leaving my duffel bag and Wolf Whacker behind, I set off down the right hand side of the tower. Making my way around its curving base, I searched for a usable opening. A decent sized hole or even a crack would be enough to accommodate my skinny chicken frame. I was pleased when I discov-

ered a large wooden door. A pair of iron braces resembling dragons ran horizontally across it. To one side of the door was a heavy, metal ring. I wasn't certain whether the ring was to be used as a knocker or if it was for pulling the door open. Just the fact that I had found a door put an end to my worries. Problem solved. In the morning, I'd knock on the door or — assuming it wasn't locked — I'd open it myself and go inside. I was

very pleased with the way things were going.

Although I couldn't use the door right this minute, I gave listening through it a try. I pressed the side of my head against the wood. At first there was nothing. Then from within the tower came the muffled sound of metal striking wood. I continued to listen and heard the shuffling of heavy footsteps. This was soon followed by the clank and clatter of objects being moved about (none too gently I might add). From the sound of things, whoever was home wasn't in a very good mood. Nonetheless, I felt better knowing that the place wasn't abandoned. I hadn't come all this way for an empty pile of stones.

Learning that the tower was occupied was a relief, but it also stirred my curiosity as to what the person or persons inside looked like. I just had to get a peek.

I poked my beak around the edges of the door in the hopes that the space between it and the wall would be enough to see inside. Unfortunately, the door fit too snugly. I lay down on my belly and tried to look under the door. From this vantage point, all I could make out was the ever so faint glow of firelight from within.

Terribly frustrated, I stood up and scratched at the ground with my clawed foot. This wasn't fair. I didn't want to have to wait until morning to have my curiosity satisfied.

Since it was still too early in the evening for me to give up, I decided

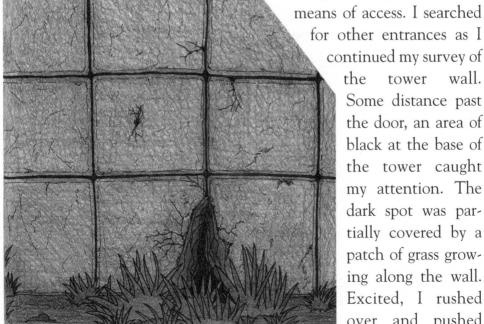

to keep looking for another means of access. I searched for other entrances as I continued my survey of the tower wall. Some distance past the door, an area of black at the base of the tower caught my attention. The dark spot was partially covered by a patch of grass growing along the wall. Excited, I rushed over and pushed away the grass. Upon closer inspection, my hopes were confirmed. There was a sizable gap between two of the stone blocks at the base of the tower. I judged it to be just wide enough for me.

Using my beak and feet, I pulled out the grass and cleared the opening. I crouched low and tightly folded my wings against my sides to squeeze into the narrow gap. This was one instance in which having a short, slender chicken body was a good thing. No fat-bellied pig boy could've made it into such a tight space. I crawled forward on my knees by using my beak to pull myself along. The tunnel was surprisingly deep. The tower's wall was several stone blocks in thickness and each block was at least twice the length of my body. In the cramped space, my wings were continuously scraping against the sides. I lost track of how many times I bumped my poor head. Ahead of me I could see the dim orange glow of firelight marking the end of the tunnel. I'd need to crawl all the way in before I could make out any details.

As I neared the end of the tunnel, I heard someone moving about inside. The source of the noise was off to the right and well out of sight. Erring on the side of caution, I proceeded more quietly. I didn't want to give myself away before knowing who or what was in there.

Reaching the end of the tunnel, I stopped to listen. There were no voices that I could make out, only a soft, grunting sound. Did the tower's occupant keep pigs inside? That would be unsanitary.

Ever so carefully, I peered through the opening and surveyed the interior. The chamber was immense, at least seventy or eighty paces from one end to the other. It had more the feeling of a great hall than a simple room. The most impressive features I saw were the large stone columns that reached to the ceiling far overhead. The columns were amazing pieces of artwork. Each had been carved with painstaking detail from a single block of white stone to resemble a flying dragon. The dragons were portrayed soaring upwards, toward the heavens. The slender dragon bodies were covered with countless scales. Their curving horns were rippled with thin, spiraling lines. Manes of stringy hair rolled down their long necks and tufts of fur dangled from their chins. Their clawed feet curled back and their eyes were wide and alive. There was a living texture to the carvings that I would have thought impossible to capture in cold stone. I found myself wishing that my eyesight weren't so poor and that there was more light so I could better appreciate the columns' beauty.

When I turned my attention away from the columns, I noticed that the chamber's floor was itself a spectacle. Thousands of perfectly cut white stone squares covered its surface. The slabs possessed a glistening pearl-like sheen that made them appear to glow. Oddly, this attractive floor was littered with sprinklings of dirt and small rocks. Strewn about were broken pieces of what had once been fine wood and metal furniture. Looking more carefully, I observed that none of the furniture was left standing. All of it had either been smashed or overturned.

What had happened here? Who would do such a thing?

I saw more signs of destruction at the far end of the chamber. Two immense, wooden cabinets, each with a dozen shelves apiece, stood against the far wall. Many of the cabinets' shelves were ripped out or badly damaged. The jars and ceramic dishes that had been on the shelves were knocked down and smashed.

Whoever lived here was either a total slob or else had a nasty temper.

Curious as to what this slovenly, mystery occupant looked like, I squeezed farther through the gap. Cautiously, I stuck my head out of the opening. I cocked my head to the right, in the direction that the sounds of movement and grunting had come from earlier. That's when I saw it.

"OH SWEET MERCIFUL BUDDHA!" I wanted to scream. One glance was enough to make me regret my curiosity. There, at the far end of the chamber, stood a great big, ugly thing. The massive, slouching brute was far taller than a man. It had nasty, bluish skin mottled with dark brown spots. The hideous creature's head was bald except for a wreath of scruffy white hair that ran from one temple to the other. Its forehead was notable for the large, orange horn sticking out of it. Thick, bushy white eyebrows hung like drooping moss over the monster's gleaming yellow eyes. From the corners of the brute's mouth, jutted two enormous, curved teeth, one on each side. One tooth pointed upwards, while the other pointed down. The thing's face was so painfully ugly I doubted whether even its own mother could love it. The clothes it wore appeared to be made from the skins of various animals. Over one shoulder was slung a gargantuan club. The crude weapon had been derived from a single massive leg bone. Whatever creature the bone had come from had been even larger than this brute.

Was this monster an ogre?

I'd heard legends and spooky tales that told of ogres ever since I was a child. They were supposed to live deep underground, usually in caverns beneath mountains. They were said to be both incredibly strong, yet, at the same time dumber than dirt. This thing fit the description. I'd always figured that ogres were simply a myth. How could such a thing exist? Then again, who'd believe a chicken curse could be real?

Not far from where the monster stood, I spied a gaping black hole in the chamber floor. Dark soil and rocks had been pushed up from below to form an earthen ring around the opening. There were more cracked floor slabs lying in the mess. A thin coating of dirt and loose stones was spread evenly across the surrounding floor. The creature must have tunneled up from beneath the tower. Was it looking for food? I hoped that it hadn't already eaten whoever was living here. I needed that person to cure me.

As I watched, the ogre rifled through a large wooden chest. Items of linen and jewelry were pulled from the chest and callously tossed aside. From within the chest, the ogre removed a shiny, black box. The box's smooth polished surface caught the flickering firelight. The monster turned its head away, shunning the glare reflecting off the box. Holding the box away from the light, the ogre pondered the object for a moment. Then the creature shook the box violently. I heard something rattle inside. The ogre gave the box a quick sniff. Determining it to be inedible, the monster tossed the box aside. The container made a heavy, clanking noise as it tumbled across the floor out of sight. The ogre again returned to its pillaging of the chest. The monster appeared to be looking for something to eat.

With the ogre suitably distracted, I braved a better look at the chamber's interior. To the ogre's right was the source of the light that illuminated the chamber. A large, decorated fireplace was set into the wall. Metalwork shaped to flow like flowering vines bordered the fireplace's polished, white stone edges. Despite the firelight's strong glow, the actual fire was small. There were but a few dwindling licks of flame and a spattering of glowing embers. I wondered how such an inadequate fire could cast so much light across such a large area. Then I noticed that it wasn't the fire that shone with such intensity, but rather the hearth. The inside of the hearth was lined with hundreds of polished silver tiles. The tiles' mirrored surfaces amplified and reflected the firelight all across the great chamber. If a decent sized fire were made, I imagined that this one fireplace could easily light the entire room.

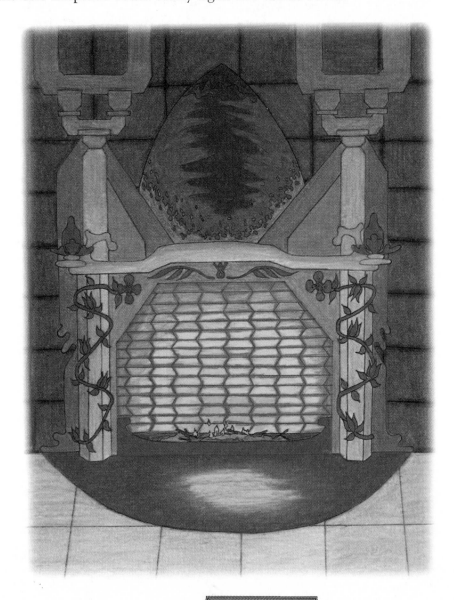

To the right, not far from the fireplace was a large, wooden table. Nearby, two chairs lay smashed and flattened on the floor. More of the ogre's doing, I figured. Still farther to the right, was an ornate marble staircase that curved upwards along the wall. Running up the side of the stairs was a stone railing carved to resemble the serpentine tail of a dragon. The staircase led tantalizingly upwards, into the heart of the tower. I wondered whether or not I should chance dashing for it. While the ogre was preoccupied down here, I could poke around upstairs. If I was fast and quiet, I was fairly certain I could make it past the brute undetected.

As I deliberated on what to do, the ogre stopped its search of the chest. Giving a loud huff, the brute raised its ugly head and sniffed the air.

I froze in place and held my breath.

"Please don't let it see me, please don't let it see me," I pleaded silently. My head with its bright red cone was sticking out of the opening. I was afraid that the ogre would spot me, but I didn't dare move. Such movement might attract the creature's attention.

Taking a few paces forward, the ogre sniffed again. This time I could see its greasy nose hairs flare in and out as it sampled the scents in the air. The beast began to growl, low and steady. Slowly it turned its head until it was looking straight at me.

"Oh Fart!" I wanted to shout. My heart raced ever faster with fear.

I'd been so caught up worrying that the monster might see me, that I hadn't considered it might be able to smell me. Too late, I remembered another interesting point about ogres that the stories had mentioned. They were reputed to posses a superb sense of smell.

The monster fixed its terrible gaze on me. The yellow eyes bored into me as I cringed within the stone gap. I did my best to shrink my head into my shoulders, like a turtle, in the hope that the monster wouldn't see me. That didn't work.

The ogre puffed up its chest as if it were getting ready to blow air. Instead, it let out a monstrous belly roar and charged at me. It grunted and snarled as it ran.

For a brief instant, my mind degenerated into hysterical panic. The

monster was huge. Its teeth were like vicious daggers and its muscular arms and legs were as thick as tree trunks. My instinct was to turn and run. Being stuck in the wall made that impossible. I couldn't go forward either. If I did, I'd be trapped in the chamber with the monster chasing after me. The only thing I could do was to scoot backwards.

I pushed off the ground with my beak and shuffled back into the tunnel as fast as I could. Before I could get very far, the ogre's big, dirty hand thrust through the opening. The monster's black fingernails scraped at the top and sides of the tunnel as they groped for me. I ducked my head low and dodged from side to side as the fingers came towards me. The powerful hand could've easily crushed my entire body with but a single squeeze. The only thing that saved me was the fact that the creature's oversized arm couldn't fit very far into the tight opening. I continued moving backwards, pushing myself along with my beak. Finally, I was able to crawl beyond the monster's reach.

The ogre roared in frustration.

I still hadn't cleared the tunnel when the brute withdrew its hand. A moment later there was a thunderous crashing noise. The wall shuddered violently and dust billowed around me from the opening in front. A second loud crash followed, then a third and a fourth. I heard chunks of stone cracking and falling to the floor. Tiny chips bounced off my head from above. The ogre couldn't reach in here because the opening was too small. It was trying to enlarge the gap with its club. The brute didn't stand a chance of succeeding. The wall was way too thick. Nevertheless, I wasn't going to wait around to be proven right. I intended to get my feathered tail out as quickly as possible. I hoped that dumb creature wouldn't realize that all it had to do was go out the front door to cut me off. The thought of being trapped in the tunnel when I turned human again scared me. I remembered being stuck in the foxhole and dreaded a repeat of the incident.

I was relieved to hear the ogre still pounding away at the wall as I wiggled out into the cool night air.

Fully freeing myself from the opening, I ran back to where I had left Wolf Whacker and my duffel bag. I didn't want to leave them where the ogre might find them. I had to hide them. The tree line was too far away for me to drag all this stuff. I needed something closer. Looking around for the nearest cover, I spotted a large patch of high grass growing at the base of the tower. I began rolling Wolf Whacker towards it. Meanwhile, the crashing sound of the ogre's club continued to echo through the night. I had lost a few feathers while backing out. The dimwitted beast must have smelt them and believed me still stuck in the wall. The monster raged away in vain. Good for it!

Pulling the last of my belongings into the brush with me, I crouched down to wait. Would the ogre come barreling out the door? I hoped not but if it did, I'd leave everything behind and head for the woods. Bye, bye silky pink underwear. Bye, bye Wolf Whacker. It's this chicken for himself.

I waited anxiously. It wasn't long before the ogre ended its assault.

Placing my head against the wall, I listened for what it was doing. A new sound came from within the tower, a scraping noise. The monster had switched from trying to batter the wall down to digging through it.

What a knob! Ogres really are dumb.

The beast grunted and scratched at the thick stone blocks. Even from outside, I could hear heavy chunks of rock crash as they were tossed aside by the beast.

I had to give the monster credit. It was relentless. Oh well! Better the brute waste its time searching for me where I wasn't than looking for me where I am.

Sometime after midnight I fell asleep to the sound of the ogre digging. I'd only meant to rest my eyes for a few minutes, but it was the next morning when I opened them again. I looked at myself and saw that I was human. In the east the sun was already over the mountains. The sky was clear. It would be a warm day. Remembering my frightening encounter with the ogre, I looked around nervously for any sign of the beast. I didn't see it anywhere. Obviously, it hadn't come out of the tower while I slept or else I wouldn't be alive.

I kept Wolf Whacker close at hand as I got dressed. I didn't want to be caught off guard in the event the ogre made a sudden appearance.

Once I was dressed, I took my duffel bag and returned to the tower door. It was still closed. Taking hold of the metal door ring, I pulled on it gently. I was being as quiet as possible in case the ogre was right inside. I hoped the hinges didn't squeak. Unfortunately, the door wouldn't budge, not even a little. Trying a second time, I pushed on it. Still, the blasted door didn't open. I tried a third time, pushing even harder. Nothing! The door had to be locked solid. I wouldn't be getting in that way. I kicked at the ground in frustration.

Discouraged, I proceeded to the gap in the wall. The opening was unchanged. For all the ogre's pounding and digging, it hadn't reached to the outside of the tower. Bending down, I peered into the small tunnel. It amazed me that I'd been able to squeeze through such a narrow opening. The tunnel was pitch black and unrevealing. Firelight was no longer visible from within the tower.

With the door not opening and the hole too small for my muscular physique, I was in a bind. It was apparent that I'd have to do some climbing in order to get inside. I took a few steps back and looked up at the tower. It stretched up and up and up. I took a few more steps back trying to see the first set of windows. They were way up on the sixth level, a long hard climb away. I sighed heavily. I was not looking forward to this. I was already seriously hungry. I hadn't eaten at all last night for fear of the ogre. My stomach was making loud gurgling noises, the kind that empty stomachs tend to make when they feel neglected. Exercise would only exacerbate my discomfort.

Before committing to the climb, I walked completely around the tower to be sure that I wasn't overlooking some easier means of entering. Finding nothing but solid wall, I resolved myself to spending the next few hours struggling up the tower's side.

I located a section of wall with good hand and footholds. I then inserted my head and one arm through the strap of my duffel bag, securing it to me. Slipping Wolf Whacker through the back of my sash, I started the climb. My fingertips and toes probed the hard stone blocks for the best grips and surest footings. As I worked my way up, I kept my chest pressed tight against the wall's cool surface.

By the time I reached the underside of the eaves that separated the first and second levels, my hands and arms were hurting. They had borne most of my body weight during the climb. Eager though I was to rest them, I was in no position to do so just yet. I first needed to get on top of the eaves.

That task would prove tricky. From the underside of the eaves I first had to climb hand over hand along one of the many wooden support beams. They were as thick as my calf and extended from the wall to the end of the eaves. When I got to the end of the beam, I then swung my legs and body up and over the eaves' outer edge and onto the tiles above. The whole effort was exhausting. After the ordeal, I lay down on the eaves and rested.

Rubbing my aching fingers, I wondered how I was going to make it the rest of the way. The builders of this tower clearly valued their headroom. It was a fair distance from one level to the next, more than five times the height of a full-grown man. Naturally, the higher up I went, the more I risked should my grip fail. Between climbs I would have to give my hands and arms plenty of time to recuperate.

Feeling that I had rested sufficiently, I started on the next level. The space between blocks was a tad wider this time around and my confidence was greater. As I climbed, I got better at choosing my hand and toeholds. Still, my

fingertips took a beating. Once I reached the next set of eaves, I allowed myself a little more time to regain my strength.

Flexing my sore fingers, I reflected on my physical state. I found myself wishing that I had some water. I hadn't had anything to drink since yesterday and the day was only going to get warmer. My mouth was getting parched and I was already starting to feel the heat. I prayed that I would find cool water and maybe even a little food when I got inside the tower. Just no ogres, please!

Glancing towards the horizon, I saw that the sun was almost half way to the midday position. If I wanted to avoid climbing during the hottest hours, I'd have to quicken my pace.

The climb to levels four and five was much the same as the others had been — long and sucky. Whatever I found in this tower, I just hoped it made up for all this trouble. The view that I was treated to from the eaves of the fifth level was of some consolation. It was spectacular. I could see out over the entire countryside. Pushing aside my thirst and hunger for a moment, I enjoyed the beauty and peace of the land. From up here I could take pleasure from the sight of nature without suffering its unpleasantness. Its dirt didn't cake my body, its sharp stones didn't stab the soles of my feet, and its insects weren't chewing on my skin. What a blessing life must be for a bird, to be above it all.

Once I had cooled down and taken my fill of the scenery, I looked to the eaves above. The first set of windows awaited me on the next level. Finally, I'd be able to set foot in the tower.

The heat of the sun's rays was making things increasingly more uncomfortable. It was time to get going. Figuring I'd do well to avoid the direct sun, I shuffled along the eaves to the backside of the tower. The tiles were slick with a coating of dust and dirt. It would've taken many years to build up such a layer. I wondered how old the tower was.

Finding shelter in the shade of the tower, my vigor quickly returned. I gave my weary arms and swollen fingers one final rub down. As I did, I looked for a section of wall with usable handholds. In short order I located a good starting point for what I hoped would be the final leg of my climb. Slipping my fingers between the blocks, I started up.

By the time I reached the base of the next set of eaves, my arms and hands were again tired. It took all of my strength to pull myself hand over hand to the outer edge of the eaves and then swing just one leg over. With a great, laborious heave-ho, I pulled up the rest of my body. Exhausted, I rolled onto my back, huffing and puffing. The smooth, cool tiles felt so refreshing. I looked at my fingertips. They were swollen and cut and throbbed with every beat of my pounding heart. Climbing had proven even harder than I'd anticipated. It was a tougher workout than even my martial training.

A faint breeze blowing in from the north offered some relief from the growing heat. The sun still hadn't reached its midday position, but the temperature was already quite warm. I was constantly wiping sweat from my forehead. Summer was a miserably hot, humid season, filled with mosquitoes and horrible rains. I hated it.

Eager to get a look inside the tower, I stood and carefully made my way over to the closest window. The tiles on this level were a grungy red and umber in color and slick underfoot. Years of layered on dust and grime had made them hazardous. The numerous piles of fresh bird poop everywhere were an added element of concern. Avoiding the doodie made

keeping a solid footing even more difficult. I thought it very odd that there should be bird poop here. I hadn't seen a single bird in the sky all morning. Wildlife avoided the area completely. They could probably sense that there was something unnatural about this hilltop.

Reaching the first window, I grabbed the rough stone edge of the windowsill to balance myself. From the ground, I'd observed that the windows were set in pairs and were shaped like sinister eyes. The window in front of me, as well as its companion a few arms' length farther down, did look like the eyes of a monster, dark and lidless. Were they supposed to resemble the eyes of the ogre? They were scary enough for the comparison. I proceeded with extreme caution. The ogre could be anywhere in the tower.

I withdrew Wolf Whacker from my sash and made ready to strike. I would jam the tip of the weapon into the first toothy blue/gray mug that jumped out at me. Leaning in closer to the window, I took a look inside. The chamber's interior was dark except for small, sunlit areas directly in front of the two sets of windows. The second set of windows lay across the chamber. The central portion of the chamber was almost pitch-black. I could barely distinguish the outlines of tables and other furniture. Leaning farther in, the air felt cold on my face and there was an odd, pungent smell.

I climbed quietly through the window. My feet made no sound as they touched down on the stone floor. In a smooth, fluid motion, I dropped to a low crouch and brought Wolf Whacker to the ready. My senses searched the gloom for the presence of a foe or hint of an attack. After a minute of quiet observation, I determined that the chamber was safe. I was alone. I moved forward, into the room's interior. Before I'd taken my third step, however, my foot sploshed into something squishy. Not bothering to inspect what it was, I wiped my foot clean on the floor and proceeded to have a look around.

The tower narrowed as it went up, making this chamber smaller than the one on the ground floor. It was barely two-thirds the size. The ceiling, however, was at least equal in height. I couldn't see precisely how high up it went. It was so dark overhead, that looking straight up was like staring into an impenetrable black void. It gave me the willies. It was impossible to know what was up there. A loathsome, hairy, bloodsucking fiend of a monster could be waiting to swoop down and drink me dry.

I tried not to think about such things. I had to stay relaxed. An overactive imagination wasn't helpful right now. I couldn't help tightening my grip on Wolf Whacker and casting frequent glances upwards as I moved deeper into the chamber.

My eyes gradually grew accustomed to the dark. I was able to distinguish the shapes of tables, stools, clay dishes, powder jars and mixing spoons. It was apparent that this chamber had once been an alchemist's lab. Four large, wooden tables occupied the central portion of the room. Various shapes and sizes of clay and metal pots sat upon the tables. More pots were stacked against the far wall. Arranged in neat rows on each of the tables were dozens of strange metal implements. There were also numerous chunky, dark stains marring the tabletops. Some of the stains looked fresh. Past the tables, I spotted two stone fire pits. The pits were round and came halfway up to my knees and were lined with unevenly shaped stones. A small dish filled with flints sat next to one of the pits. Near the dish was a dust-covered clay jar. I bent down and picked it up. Shaking the jar, I could hear the swishing of liquid.

Was it water? If it was, I was drinking it no matter how old or stale it might be. I was so parched I felt as if I'd gargled with sand.

Popping the jar's wooden plug, I took a whiff of its contents. From the smell, I knew that this stuff wouldn't quench my thirst. The jar was filled with lamp oil. Did the tower's owners use this in combination with the flints to start fires? If they did, it wasn't a very magical method.

As I walked about the chamber, I got the impression that whoever had lived here, simply up and left one day. Everything was in place, ready to be used. Yet, from the thickness of the dust and the amount of cobwebs, the tower's occupants had been gone many years. Then there was the matter of the bitter chemical stench. It was stronger here in the middle of the room. I couldn't put my finger on what it was, but I knew I didn't like it.

Focusing my attention on a darkened section of the chamber wall, I noticed a shadowy outline. Peering closer, I saw that I was looking at a pair of large shelf cases. With so little light to see by, it didn't surprise me that I hadn't noticed them until now. I walked towards the cases. Each shelf was stocked with earthen jars, wooden bowls and small metal pots. I took a jar from one of the shelves and looked inside. It was filled with a finely ground powder. I confirmed this by taking a pinch from the jar and running the substance between my fingers. Sniffing the powder, I discovered that it was odorless. I wiped the powder from my fingers and returned the jar to the shelf. I grabbed another jar. Methodically, I examined jar after jar to learn what they contained. What I found were more powders, chunks of rock and bits of crystals. Moving on to the pots, I discovered a wide variety of very smelly roots and herbs. This was all the stuff a wacky alchemist would need.

To the right of the shelf cases were a pair of long robes. They hung from pegs imbedded into the wall. Even in the dim light, I could tell that they were brightly colored. I touched the fabric of one robe, running the material between my fingers. There was a thick layer of dust on it, but it was still splendidly soft. The tower's owner must've been rich to afford such luxurious garments. Why were these beautiful things left behind?

I started to eye the second robe when I noticed another shadowy section of wall to the right of it. That portion of the chamber was especially dark. It remained untouched by the light coming in from the windows. Seeing an irregular shape in the blackness, I stepped closer. I squinted and reached for the shape. My hand touched on something cold and metallic. I felt around a bit more. My fingers ran over the grainy texture of wood. Closing my eyes for a few moments, I forced them to better adjust to the dark. When I reopened them, I could see that my hand was touching a wooden door. There was a pair of sturdy iron braces set horizontally across it for added strength. It was similar in style to the main door of the tower on the ground floor. I was shocked that I hadn't seen the door right away. When I had looked in this direction earlier, I'd missed it completely. I looked around to see if maybe I had missed any other doors. The rest of the chamber was better lit, and I saw no other ways in or out of the room. This door was the only one. That meant that the staircase I'd seen last night had to be on the other side. The stairs would connect me to the other levels of the tower. I wouldn't have to do anymore climbing. I was thrilled, but restrained myself from shouting a cheer. The ogre could well be on the other side of the door.

I grasped the door ring and gave it an ever so gentle tug. The door failed to open. I tried again, a little harder this time. Still, it didn't open. Taking a step back, I looked the door over. I felt like an idiot when I saw that the locking bolts were still secured.

"Okay, dunce, it would help if you unlocked the thing first," I berated myself in a low voice.

Pulling back the bolts, I tried the door again. Once more it failed to open. Frustrated, I stepped away from the door and checked for any other deadbolts. I saw none. The door was unlocked. I didn't understand why it wasn't opening. What was wrong? I gave the door a final tug, as hard as I could, with no result. The door had to be jammed, possibly from the other side. I knew I'd never be able to kick the thing down. It was much too strong. Exasperated, I decided to come back to the problem after I had finished exploring the rest of the room.

Returning to the center of the chamber, I passed between two of the tables. As I marveled at the many tiny tools I saw on one of the tables, my foot landed in another squishy mess on the floor. This time, I stopped to investigate. Bending down to see, I looked at the substance. There wasn't enough light to make out its color. All I could tell was that it was thick and chunky. I also learned from my close proximity that it stunk. It was the same bitter smell that filled the entire chamber; only this stuff was much more intense.

Wiping my foot clean of the filth, I stood up and looked around. All over the floor were dozens, if not hundreds of similar goo spots. Some were old and dried out, while still others appeared to be fresh and juicy. Looking at the tabletops again, I realized that what I'd mistaken earlier for globby stains, were in fact more of the smelly goo plops.

What is this stuff? My apprehension grew stronger. The droppings looked like the bird poop on the eaves. Had birds made this mess? I didn't see any feathers anywhere.

A soft rustling noise from overhead caught my attention.

"This can't be good," I whispered as I looked up at the ceiling. Through the inky blackness, I could see nothing. What I needed was a lamp.

Searching about for something to use, I remembered the dish of flints. Hurrying to the dish, I set my duffel bag and Wolf Whacker down on the floor. I pulled out the two best flints from the dish. Now what I needed was something to set on fire.

At the edge of the table behind me I spotted a wooden stirring spoon. Grabbing it off the table, I dipped it into the container of oil that I had found earlier. The thick oil oozed down the handle of the spoon, slowly making its way to my hand. I tilted the spoon so that the oil wouldn't get on me. Setting the spoon down on the edge of the fire pit, I held the flints over it and began striking them together. Tiny sparks flew off the stones with each impact, but none were big enough to ignite the oil.

From above me, there were more sounds of movement. Fearing that my activity was stirring up something unfriendly, I hurried to light the fire.

At last a large enough spark struck the oil, igniting it. Grasping the spoon's handle, I held it up towards the ceiling. Drops of flaming oil dripped, landing at my feet. Moving the makeshift torch from side to side, I searched for the source of the noises.

Suddenly, a sharp-pitched screech rang throughout the chamber. The sound was frightening as it echoed again and again.

My fear intensified. What the

heck was up there?

Even with the torchlight, I couldn't see a thing. The ceiling was too high and the room too dark. The torch was useless.

Another shriek echoed from overhead.

In desperation, I flung the burning spoon towards the ceiling. It arched up, partially illuminating what was overhead. Through the swirl of firelight, I made out a jumble of wood beams that crisscrossed the ceiling. Amongst the beams were interspersed tiny flickering pricks of reddish light that twinkled as the firelight caught them. On its way down, the torch struck one of the beams and made a loud clatter. Suddenly, the ceiling came alive with shadowy shapes that fluttered about wildly. For a brief instant, the light of the falling torch showed me what the shapes were.

BATS! A whole honking nest of dirty, ugly bats were right above my head. Bat poop was what covered the tables and floor and stunk up the chamber.

Disturbed by the light of the torch, the enraged bats dropped from their perches and descended towards me.

Freaked, I scooped up my duffel bag and staff and ran for the nearest window.

The bats were right behind me. Several flew past me even as I dove in blind panic headfirst out the window. I belly-flopped onto the eaves with a hard, gut-busting thud. This knocked the wind out of me, but I had no time to dwell on it. My momentum was carrying me down the slope of the eaves. I was but a second away from plunging to my death. In desperation, I swung my duffel bag towards the carved stone figure of a dragon that sat on the edge of the eaves. By a miracle, part of the bag strap looped around the figure. The bag itself caught underneath the lip of the eaves. All this happened as I went headfirst over the side. I held tight to the bag strap with one hand. My fall was halted with an abrupt snap. In reflex, I squeezed the bag strap harder. My body was sent swinging back and forth.

There I was, dangling six stories above the ground. I held Wolf Whacker in one hand, while maintaining a death-grip on the strap of the bag with the other. It was at this time that I learned how truly fast my heart could race without bursting. My heartbeat thundered in my ears like the great bull-drum from my valley.

Overhead, the bats fluttered about in a frenzied mass of leather wings and pointy ears. They were agitated but didn't attack. The bats circled the tower twice, squealing and shrieking. Then, without showing me the least bit of interest, they flew back in through the window.

I breathed a sigh of relief

as the last bat returned to the tower. I'd been such a fool. The bats hadn't been hostile at all, just startled. I'd nearly killed myself running away from a bunch of little animals that were as scared of me as I was of them. I could've avoided all this excitement, if I'd simply reacted calmly instead of succumbing to mind-bungling hysteria. Further self-recriminations had to wait. The strap of my bag was beginning to strain under my weight. Placing Wolf Whacker between my teeth to free up one hand, I reached up and grabbed the edge of the eaves. Grunting and groaning from the effort, I pulled myself up. Still jittery and unsure of my balance, I remained on my hands and knees as I crawled back up towards the tower wall. When I got there, I propped myself against the cool stone blocks and paused to gather my wits.

It was several minutes before my heart ceased its efforts to pound its way out of my chest. When I was ready to stand up, I did so far from the window. I wasn't going to push my luck by going back into the alchemy chamber. I didn't fancy seeing those pug-faced bats anymore than they wanted to see me. We obviously creeped one another out. Since the chamber door wouldn't open, I had no reason to linger here anyway. I would have to try to access the stairs from the next level. It had windows too, and hopefully a working door. Right now, I preferred climbing to bats.

I was extra cautious as I made my way to level seven. Having nearly fallen to my death once, I'd learned the folly of taking the dangers of the situation too lightly. I wasn't going to be careless a second time.

Upon reaching the next level, I discovered to my surprise, that this wasn't the top of the tower as I'd originally thought. There was, in fact, another level above it. Yesterday when I'd counted the levels, I had missed seeing it.

"An eighth level?" I said, shaking my head in dismay. This tower was enormous. I couldn't imagine any building in the world being this high.

Far above my head was the bottom of a balcony. Wood floorboards and colorful support beams ran beneath it. I looked forward to going up there. Something told me it would be worthwhile.

My exploration of the seventh level proved a major disappointment. The chamber turned out to be nothing but a library. Large bookcases, crammed with old books, lined the wall. In addition, I was loathe to discover more sleeping bats in the rafters. This time I was careful not to disturb the nasty little curs.

I enjoyed reading, so the discovery of a room full of books would normally have excited me. One of the books might have held a clue on how to rid me of the curse. Unfortunately, whatever knowledge was contained within the hundreds upon hundreds of volumes was inaccessible to me. Every book I looked at had been written in some unknown form of writing. To make matters worse, there weren't even any pictures.

Why couldn't this have been a kitchen? I was so hungry and thirsty I could cry. I can't drink a good book.

The chamber's single door proved as useless as the books. The crummy thing wouldn't open even after I had unbolted it. Like the door in the alchemy lab, it, too was jammed. One difference I picked up on right away was that the wood of this door was splintered and cracked in several places. Clearly someone had tried to break into the room from the outside.

Throwing subtlety aside, I tried forcing the door open. I pulled it, I pushed it, I kicked it and I cursed it. It wouldn't budge. Finally, I figured out why my efforts were unsuccessful. The hinges were damaged. Whatever had tried to break through had bent the hinges inward to the extent that they no longer functioned.

Had the ogre done this? What a bummer!

Coming up disappointed at every turn thus far, I left the library feeling sullen.

Sitting on a windowsill, I looked out over the green, forest-covered land. It was past midday. The sun was high and bright, in contrast to my depressed spirits. The refreshing breeze that had been blowing since midmorning was doing little to improve my mood. My throat was as dry as an old bone. If I didn't get some water soon, I would have to climb back down. First, I was going to explore that top level. I'd come too far to quit now. The next chamber could well hold the cure that I was after. Even if it didn't, at least there might be something to eat or drink.

Eager to get the climb over with, I started up. Being so near to the top actually made the going easier. The inward incline at this point was such, that instead of having to go practically straight up, I was now ascending at a slope. This took a lot of the pressure off my tired fingers.

Reaching the underside of the balcony, I paused to assess the final portion of the climb. Just above my head were the balcony's floorboards. The colorful beams that supported them were within arm's reach. Each beam was painted with pictures of dragons and extended from the tower wall to the end of the balcony.

Letting go of the wall and grabbing hold of a support beam had always been the trickiest part of getting onto the eaves. The wood was usually very dusty, making it difficult to hold onto the curved beam. In this case, it was going to be even harder. The beams under the balcony were twice as long as the ones holding up the eaves. Crossing them would sorely tax my hands. I asked my ancestors for the strength to see me through safely.

Sliding along the wall, I positioned myself directly under the nearest beam. I verified that Wolf Whacker and my duffel bag were still secure and in no danger of falling. I then got on with the most dangerous part of the climb. Reaching out with one hand, I grabbed hold of the beam. The thick layer of dust on it caused my first attempt to fail. Quickly, I tried again and secured my grip. Taking a deep breath, I then jumped clear of the tower wall and grabbed the beam with my other hand.

For a moment I hung free, my legs swaying back and forth. I hurried to establish a better hold on the beam. It was fortunate for me that there were no splinters in the wood. Making my first hand change off, then my second, I climbed in increments along the length of the beam. I kept my

motions smooth and my legs as still as possible. The more my body swayed, the more stress it put on my hands.

I'd gotten half way across, when I made the mistake of looking down. I was terrified to see how much emptiness separated my dangling feet from the ground below. I had never been this far from solid ground before and I can honestly say that I didn't care for it at all. It wasn't the same as looking over the side of a tall cliff. Then my feet were planted firmly on rock and earth. Here, there was nothing but empty space beneath. I was left further humbled by the endless stretches of land that were spread out before me. The altitude soon out-shadowed the grandeur and began to sour my stomach. I thought for a moment that I might get sick. Fortunately, having had nothing to eat all day left me with nothing to throw up. I swallowed hard and forced my eyes to focus only on the end of the beam. I then willed my hands to move. The left hand first, and then the right, then the left again. I had to hurry. My muscles were fatigued. They wouldn't last much longer.

At that moment, the wind seemed to sense my torment and sent a strong gust to buffet me. I ignored the jostling and kept going. My hands were trembling as I reached the ledge of the balcony. I wasted no time in swinging my legs between the railings and pulled myself up. With this exhausting endeavor done, I collapsed flat on my belly and caught my breath. After a minute, I rose to my elbows and slowly, painfully, opened and closed my hands. They trembled as I worked them. At first, they were slow to respond. Gradually, as their strength returned they began to move more freely.

While I recuperated, I reflected on how close and how often I'd come to dying today.

"Never again," I swore out loud. Never would I do anything as insane as this climb.

I rolled over and sat up, placing both hands on the balcony's wooden deck for support and reassurance. I still wasn't ready to stand. All I had the energy for was sitting there and enjoying the exquisite view that my toil and sweat had purchased. I wasn't disappointed. I had thought the views from the lower level eaves spectacular, but what I saw from up here put them to shame. It was like looking down from the clouds.

The rich light and dark greens of the countryside went on forever. The entire kingdom of Koguryo seemed to be laid out before me. I was certain that were my eyes not so poor, I might've even seen all the way to the Eastern Sea, perhaps even the southern kingdoms of Shilla, Paekche and Kaya.

When I'd finished appreciating the scenery, I turned my attention towards the tower and balcony. The balcony I was on appeared to extend all the way around the tower. From the tower's wall to the balcony's edge, it was a good ten paces. A wooden guardrail ran the entire length. An unusual feature, which I couldn't explain, were the vertical iron rods set at even intervals along the railing. Each rod was twice as tall as I was and topped with a flat copper fitting. I couldn't tell what purpose they might serve, only that they weren't attractive enough to be decorations.

Of greater interest to me than the funky balcony fixtures was the entrance to the tower. There was no door — only a simple, red curtain drawn across the open entryway. The fabric of the curtain was old. Its color had faded due to exposure to the elements and its edges were badly frayed. I considered the possibility that the ogre could be hiding behind it. I vowed not to be caught off guard. Standing up, I reached back and pulled Wolf Whacker from my sash. Cautiously, I walked forward. I pointed the tip of my staff at the entrance, ready to jab it into the eye of anything that jumped out at me.

Suddenly, from within the tower, I heard a man's gruff voice shout, "You! Who are you out there?"

Startled, I nearly jumped backwards off the balcony. If not for the railing, I would've surely gone over the side.

I recomposed myself as quickly as I could and took up a fighting stance. Cementing my courage, I walked towards the curtain. I called out to the owner of the voice using the most masculine, intimidating tone I could manage, "Hello inside."

"I didn't ask for a greeting. I asked who you are," the grainy voice scolded.

Cautiously, I pulled back the curtain. There was no one hiding behind it, so I stepped through. I glanced about the chamber. The place

appeared empty. Where was the owner of the voice? Had it been a ghost that called out to me, or perhaps, an invisible, flesh-eating demon?

Nervously, I took a few tentative steps towards the center of the chamber. There were nine wooden columns in the middle of the room, each nearly as wide as my shoulders. I circled slightly to one side of the columns and saw no one lurking behind them. As for furniture to hide behind, there was very little. A chair, a small table and a few wooden buckets were all that was left. The remainder of the furnishings was at the far end of the chamber. They'd been used to erect a sloppy barricade against the room's only door.

My suspicions grew. The furniture hadn't just walked over there by itself. Someone in here had to have moved it.

I began to get a creepy feeling as if I were being watched. I was reminded of how the wolves had stalked me through the forest, tracking me, always keeping just out of sight. I felt certain that someone was watching me now.

I tightened my grip on Wolf Whacker and once again scanned the room for danger. I still saw no one. I wondered whether or not I should call out again, or wait for whoever was here to make the first move. I took a few more steps towards the center of the room. My eyes scanned back and forth.

This was the smallest chamber I'd seen so far. Its general shape was similar to the others. It had a single, rounded wall that sloped inward the farther up it went. The ceiling, however, was different. It was much higher than those of the other chambers, perhaps twice as high. Midway up, there were nine, black beams set perpendicular to the wall. The beams met together in the center, forming a star pattern. In the middle of this pattern was something that appeared similar to a giant wagon wheel. The "wheel" was copper colored and very heavy looking. It was composed of a large outer ring and a smaller, solid inner circle. Slender spokes connected the two together. The black beams were connected to the outer portion of the "wheel" by thick, metal rings. At the center of the inner circle was a vertical iron rod like the ones I'd seen along the rail of the balcony. However, this rod was at least three to four times longer than those outside. The base was secured to the center of the copper "wheel" while the far end reached all the way to the ceiling. The nine columns in the central portion of the room each touched one of the black beams overhead. As best I could tell, neither the black beams nor the columns were load-bearing supports. They didn't seem strong enough. The weight of the enormously high ceiling appeared to be borne solely by its domed ceiling and nine stone arches. These arches were aligned with and extended down to the black beams. Each arch was inset with a deep, sharp-edged groove that began where the arch met the beams. This groove ran almost the entire length of the arch. The creamy-white tiles of the dome set them apart from the gray blocks of the chamber wall.

The main source of light for the chamber came from dozens of lit candles placed in decorative brass holders on the columns. These provided the room with an ample supply of flickering firelight.

What I found most interesting were the tapestries lining the wall. There must have been over twenty of them (I didn't take the time to do an exact count). They covered almost the entire surface of the wall. Each portrayed in vibrant colors, a different scene. When I looked at them as a whole, I realized that they were all part of a larger story.

I glanced at the tapestries and attempted to decipher the overall plot from the many separate images. What I understood of the story was this: when the world was far younger than it is now, a monster of great darkness arose from within the earth. It was a really ugly cuss, with horns and fangs and gnarly red hair that grew in thick tufts out of some not so nice places. The Dark Monster unleashed all sorts of unnatural forces upon both nature and man. Then, in the heavens there appeared a blinding white light. From this light emerged twelve strangely dressed men and women. The Twelve descended to earth to wage war against The Dark Monster, using the powerful magics at their disposal. Joining the Twelve in their cause, were a host of exotic dragons. These magnificent creatures came in an endless variety of shapes and colors. Although portrayed on simple cloth, their rainbow-colored, scaled bodies seemed to glisten as if real. Some dragons were pictured with great, sweeping wings, others had small wings or none at all. Some had horns while others didn't. The bodies of many were long and slender; others were stocky and powerful. Many had fiery manes and long, streaking whiskers. These majestic creatures fought alongside The Twelve against the hordes of otherworldly beasts unleashed by The Dark Monster to do its bidding.

Most of the tapestry scenes were depictions of separate engagements between these two forces. As war raged over the land, in the skies and under the water, many great and terrible deeds were done.

In the final scenes of the story, The Twelve and their dragon allies met The Dark Monster and its ugly demon minions in a horrific battle. The Twelve carried several small objects into the battle that were vaguely depicted as being surrounded by auras of light. Using these mystical objects, The Twelve defeated the demon army and bound its master in chains of light. The very last tapestry showed The Dark Monster being imprisoned by The Twelve, behind a glowing white gate. The key to sealing the gate seemed to be a large staff that three

of The Twelve held in unison. At this point, the story ended.

I found the tale exciting and wondered why I'd never heard of it. Was it so old that no one living recalled it?

I stepped closer to one of the tapestries to examine it in more detail. It was then that I noticed the strange symbols along the edge. From a distance, I'd thought they were just a part of the border design, an artistic feature. Now I saw that it was in fact a form of writing. It was the same strange writing system found in the books in the library. The symbols filled the borders of all the tapestries. Was this the text that accompanied the story?

"Well, Boy, are you deaf…or just dumb? Why don't you answer?" shouted an angry voice from behind me.

Distracted by the tapestries, I'd completely forgotten about there being someone else in here. With a surprised hop, I turned and faced in the direction of the voice.

Out from behind one of the tapestries to my left stepped a skinny, old man. His face was lean and wrinkled and aside from the tufts of bushy white hair above his ears, he was entirely bald. The old guy's broad, grizzled chin was stubbled with whiskers and on the left side of it was a hideous black wart the size of a horse fly. The sight of it turned my stomach. Disturbingly, my eyes refused to look away from the disgusting thing.

"Well, who are you, Boy?" the old man insisted.

Still staring uncontrollably at his gigantic wart, I didn't answer. The old man's pushy demeanor belied his runty stature. Hunched forward on a bamboo cane, he stood barely as high as my shoulders. When he took a few steps towards me, the cane was the only thing that kept his frail body upright.

The old man's clothes were of simple design: loose fitting and tied in the front across the chest. He wore a gray coat with tan trim that hung in loose, baggy folds over his skinny frame. He looked like a child who had put on his father's clothes. Slung across his chest was a large cloth pouch that hung at his side. Upon his baldhead he wore a small blue and green hat, of a style that looked quite strange to me.

Hobbling a few steps closer, the old man stopped in front of me. There was a deep, accusatory scowl etched into his wrinkled face. Clearly, he didn't welcome my being here.

"Once more, Boy, who are you? You're obviously a dimwit who has trouble answering questions."

"I'm sorry. I saw no one when I came in. I thought perhaps it was a ghost that had called to me," I said in my own defense.

"A ghost? Ha!" the old man scoffed dismissively. He quickly fired off more questions in rapid succession. "What's your name, Boy? What are you doing here? And how did you get in?"

I didn't like the rude tone of the old man's questions and even though I shouldn't have, I responded with sarcasm instead of respect. "Do you want those questions answered in order? Because if you do, then you're going to have to repeat the second one, I didn't catch it. Your mumbling and spitting distracted me."

"Insolent child! You're a fool for coming here. Who are you?" the old man snapped angrily. His face turned a bright red and his scowl deepened to the extent that his eyebrows now practically touched.

"My name is Kang Goo-shu. I came to this tower looking for help."

"Help?" the old man balked at the word. "I'm afraid I'm in no position to be of help. In fact, I'm in need of rescuing myself. And you will be too, if the ogre gets through that door tonight." He pointed with his cane at the barricaded door across the room.

The furniture he'd piled against it was lightweight: three chairs, a small table and a number of urns. My wussy little brother could've shoved the lot of it aside without breaking a sweat. The old guy was deluding himself if he thought he'd keep the monster out with such a flimsy barricade.

"Last night, that cave-dwelling nuisance smashed around downstairs for a few hours. It then came up here again and tried to force the door. The dawn finally drove it off," the old man said.

"The dawn?" I asked. What was the connection between the ogre and dawn?

I waited for a reply, but the old man offered none.

"Excuse me, Sir, but those things you have piled against the door aren't going to keep out the ogre. I've seen the brute. It's huge and has a big, really big club."

"You impertinent, opinionated whelp of a child, I know that already." Bits of spittle flew from the grouchy old man's mouth.

I took a step back to avoid the shower.

"That blue devil showed up three days ago. Burrowed right up under the floor, it did. One minute I was sitting down having dinner, the next, floor tiles and dirt were being thrown everywhere." The old man swung his cane about wildly simulating the action.

"I barely got upstairs before that filthy monster climbed out of the hole. I've been stuck here in the observatory ever since."

"So this chamber is an observatory," I said. Until now, I hadn't known what its purpose was. I'd planned to refer to it as the tapestry room. But why would the old man come up here to hide? An observatory wasn't going to be stocked with food or water or weapons. It made no sense.

"Sir, why would you remain in the tower with an ogre running around downstairs? You should've run into the woods and hid the moment it appeared."

"Ha!" the old man guffawed. "That would've been just the advice to follow if my goal were to be eaten." He laughed again, this time much louder.

The old man took a step closer and pushed his face towards mine. "Me? Out there in the woods at night? Between the ogre and me, which of us do you think can see better in the dark, huh? Or has a better sense of hearing or smell?" He started to laugh again but it quickly turned into a series of wet, throaty coughs. The old man clutched tightly at his chest until the fit finally passed. Recovering his breath, he sneered and said, "Even a simpleton like you shouldn't require more than one guess as to which of us is the faster runner."

The old coot snickered as he looked me up and down, "From the looks of you, you're an ignorant farm boy. You know nothing of ogres and their ways."

"I know enough not to trap myself in a place where I can't get out, but the ogre can still get in," I retorted.

The old man gave a disapproving huff and turned his back. Mumbling unpleasant things about me under his breath, he hobbled to the nearby chair. His ancient joints creaked like rusted hinges as he lowered himself into the seat. Once he'd made himself comfortable, he looked at me. In a tired, unenthusiastic voice he said, "Tell me again, Boy, what's your name?"

"It's not 'Boy,' I'll tell you that much," I said, having grown annoyed with the old coot's impolite way of addressing me. I'd been taught to be respectful of my elders, but this guy was the rudest person I'd ever met.

"My name is Kang Goo-shu," I said brusquely.

The old man opened his mouth to speak again, but I held my hand up to interrupt him.

"Excuse me, Sir," I said speaking as politely as I could in view of how much I disliked him. "I'm terribly thirsty after climbing the tower. Might you by chance have some water?"

Irritated by the interruption, the old man threw a bony thumb over his shoulder. "Behind me is a jug of water," he indicated. "Have some if it'll bring you better manners."

I bowed halfheartedly to the old man and hurried to where he had pointed. On the floor near the wall I spotted a bucket nearly full of water. Dropping my duffel bag and staff, I fell to my knees and eagerly scooped up a handful of water. I drank it down as fast as I could. The water tasted funny, salty or something.

"Blind, deaf idiot," the old man shouted.

I turned back to see why he was yelling.

The old man was struggling to rise from his chair. When he finally did, he shook a knobby fist at me and shouted, "That's my wash water, imbecile. Can't you tell a jug from a bucket? The water jug is over there." He pointed to a brown clay jug sitting on the floor to my right.

Disgusted, I spat out as much of the bath water taste from my mouth as I could. I then ran to the water jug and took a big swig from it. After thoroughly swishing the water around in my mouth, I spat it out. I prayed to the sacred spirits of my ancestors for the strength to survive this humiliation.

Bemused by my torment, the old man chuckled and sat back down. "What is it you came here seeking help for, Kang Goo-shu?" he asked.

I took a big drink of water from the jug and walked over to the old man, keeping the jug with me.

"I thought there might be a sorcerer here with the power to remove a curse," I said, drinking more of the water.

The old man raised a bushy eyebrow. The mention of a curse had piqued his curiosity.

"What sort of curse?" he asked.

I hesitated to say any more. This old grouch couldn't even get past the ogre downstairs. How could he possibly help me? And if he couldn't help me, then why should I share with him the details of my shame?

Seeing my reluctance, the short-tempered old geezer struck the floor with the end of his cane impatiently, "I asked you, what curse? Tell me."

Angered by his pressing, I shouted back, "A chicken curse, Old Man. Chicken! Chicken! Chicken! Chicken!"

The old man's response surprised me. Instead of looking confused or surprised, he appeared amused. This made me even angrier. "What're you grinning about, you old goat?" I yelled "There's nothing funny about any of this."

"So you're one of those wretched chicken boys from that cursed valley east of here, eh?"

I took a half step back in shock and nearly dropped the water jug. "You know of my valley? And the curse?"

The old man laughed. "Of course I do. That curse is well known."

"By whom?" I asked, in amazement. Both villages kept the curse a secret from outsiders.

"By we who practice and follow the old arts. By those of us still alive with knowledge of the Mang-Wi," the old man said.

"The Mang-Who?"

"Not Mang-Who you nit! The Mang-Wi. They're the ancient magic wielders whom you have to thank for the wondrous tower in which you now stand. They're also the source of the magic forces behind your curse."

"Splendid. When I see these Mang-goos, I'll be sure to tell them how impressed I am by their craftsmanship. Maybe after some hefty sucking up, they'll be kind enough to remove this curse from me."

"Good luck finding them. They're all long gone. Long, long gone." The old man made a laughing sound that resembled an owl hooting. Delivering bad news must be how he got his jollies.

"Of course they are," I threw my hands up in frustration. I felt defeated. There went my only chance for a normal life.

"I only said the Mang-Wi were gone, you silly boy, I didn't say their art was. As I mentioned, there are those of us who still study the old magics. I…happen to be one of them." The old man held his whiskered chin up proudly. This made the ugly wart on his face stand out even more prominently.

"Then you can help me?" I asked, my hope rising again.

The old man's proud expression inverted to a rigid frown. He turned his head to the side as if by doing so, he could avoid the question. After a pause he admitted reluctantly, "I'm afraid not. While it is true that I'm a practitioner of the Mang-Wi arts, the fact is that I haven't the power to remove such a powerful curse. The old witch who cursed your village over a century ago was an awesome creature. Her name was Lang-shie and her knowledge of the Dark One's arts was great. Your ancestors were fools to have earned her wrath. The chicken curse is a bad one, for sure."

"No kidding?" I mumbled to myself. I didn't need a history lesson from this guy. And I sure didn't need him telling me how stupid those two boys had been all those years ago. I was living proof of the consequences of their ill-conceived actions.

"You are a sorcerer, aren't you?" I asked, pressing the old man.

"A sorcerer? Well, yes…I'm a sorcerer…" he said with hesitation. "after a fashion…"

"After a fashion? What does that mean?"

The old man squirmed in his chair uncomfortably.

"Are you a sorcerer, or aren't you?"

The old man grew irritated. "All right, yes, I am a sorcerer."

"Then is there anything you know of that can help me?"

The old man rested both hands atop his cane and leaned forward. "I know the spell that would cure you. I have memorized the ancient incantations. However, without the otherworldly power of the Mang-Wi, it's no use. It's a simple question of power, Boy. I haven't enough of it to remove the chicken curse from you. I don't know anyone alive who could. It would take an incredible command of the Mang-Wi arts. The dark energies cursing you would have to be channeled away and their mystic lease in this world rescinded. Compared to what you ask of me, the casting of the original curse was mere child's play. My powers are limited. I'm capable of preparing a few potions, making fire spring from the air and a short-term levitation spell. These are the extent of my abilities."

"Levitate? So you can fly?" I asked in amazement.

"No, fool, I can't fly. I said levitate. I can float straight up then lower myself back down again. I don't swoosh back and forth through the air. I used a levitation spell to reach this observatory after sealing off the two levels below. It's a very demanding spell and its effects are extremely draining. I'm still worn out from the exertion."

So this old sorcerer was responsible for securing the dead bolts on the doors downstairs. By levitating, he had been able to move via the windows between the alchemy lab and library before floating up here. I wished that I could have levitated. That would've been a lot easier than scratching and clawing my way up the wall.

The old man sat, looking dejected. "I haven't even enough power to invoke protection spells to safeguard me from the ogre. If it weren't for the Mang-Wi enchantments already on the doors, I'd be in the monster's belly by now."

Tired of standing, I seated myself in front of the sorcerer and folded my legs. Hearing him list the things he couldn't do was getting boring. I decided to change the topic and maybe get some useful information.

"What was that you mentioned earlier about the dawn driving the ogre away?"

The old man shifted in his seat. My abrupt change of subject had annoyed him. Nevertheless, he answered, "Ogres are creatures of darkness. They can't abide sunlight."

"Well, if the ogre doesn't like sunlight, why haven't you simply walked out of here during the day? Does it sleep below in the tower?"

"No, silly boy, ogres prefer the damp of a musty old cave to man-made dwellings. Deep underground is the only place they instinctively feel safe during daylight hours." There was an enthusiastic glint in the old man's eyes as he spoke about the ogre and its weakness. The sorcerer's practical skills were admittedly lacking, but now he was being afforded an opportunity to show off his extensive book-

knowledge. This was a topic he felt more confident discussing.

"The ogre returns to its lair just before sunrise each day. The reason I haven't left the tower is because of…" the old sorcerer hesitated, as if finishing the sentence might have revealed too much. His private plans were obviously not on the table for discussion. This piqued my curiosity as to what the sorcerer was doing here.

"What brought you here?" I asked.

The old man pretended not to have heard me.

I repeated the question a second time, only louder. This time he answered.

"I'm looking for something."

"What sort of something?"

"A magical something," his dry voice raised a notch. "It's a small item, nothing of importance." He waved his hands as if the gesture alone could dismiss the item's significance. "As I said before, I'm a practitioner of the old magics. For that reason, I collect certain things, things that posses magical properties. I believe that this tower and the others like it might yet hold knowledge and mystical artifacts. I've spent my whole life searching for them."

The old sorcerer's mention of other towers intrigued me. I'd be sure to ask about them later. For now, I wanted to learn his true reason for coming here. I didn't buy the explanation he'd given. The old fox was looking for something all right, but it had to be of importance. There was no way he'd stay stuck up here for three days with an angry ogre outside the door if what he was after was of little value. Whatever he was looking for had to be powerful. It might even be of help to me. I wagered the old sorcerer could probably do with some help.

Feigning disappointment, I shook my head. "I wasted days just trying to find this tower. So there is nothing you know of that might help rid me of my curse?"

The old man huffed. "I know of an incantation. But as I told you, I don't have the power to reverse the curse completely."

Making a show of it, I picked up my duffel bag and staff and stood up as if to leave. "Well, if there's nothing you can do for me, I might as well get going. I don't know how you're going to get rid of that ogre and find your unimportant magical item, Sir, but good luck to you."

I turned and started for the balcony. Hopefully, the sorcerer would realize that this was his last chance to elicit my help and offer me something — a clue, even a hint at a cure.

My deception paid off. The old sorcerer hurriedly held up a bony finger and shouted, "Now wait a minute, Boy. There's no need for you to leave just yet. You must be hungry. Have some of these." The old man's fingers fumbled through the cloth pouch at his side. From it he pulled out several roasted chestnuts and offered them to me.

Trying to appear reluctant, I begrudgingly accepted the chestnuts and offered a short bow in gratitude. I then dropped my staff and bag on the floor and sat down. I began eagerly peeling the husks from the nuts and popping the meat into my mouth.

The old sorcerer watched me eat for a moment. Seeing that my apparent impatience to leave had been placated, he leaned in towards me and cleared his throat to get my attention. When I looked up, he started to speak. His voice was all but a hushed whisper, as though he feared someone might be listening. "On the lowest level of this tower, there is a magic item. It might be of help to you." A glint of excitement flashed in the old man's eyes. It unnerved me. It was the same glint my younger brother, Young-seoul, would get when he was plotting ways to get me into trouble with our father.

"What is this item?" I asked suspiciously.

"It's a golden disc imbued with tremendous energies. It's downstairs being hovered over by that dreadful ogre. I haven't been able to get anywhere near it since that monster showed up."

"Is this the same item you spoke of before? The one you said wasn't important?" I said, allowing my suspicions to show.

The old sorcerer gave a shrug with his knobby shoulders. "I didn't know if I could trust you before," he said frankly, "but now I see my earlier caution was unnecessary. I find you to be a good and honest boy. I know you'd never try to cheat or hurt an old man." His attempt at a sincere grin was frightening. The sight of those brown teeth was off-putting and I had to look away.

"I can confide in you, can't I?" he asked me.

"Sure," I said trying to sound innocent.

The sorcerer leaned in even closer, bringing his nasty smile practically up to my face. "If you disposed of the ogre for me, I could use the power of the disc to remove at least part of the curse from you," he said.

Hearing this, I nearly gagged on the chestnut I was eating. "Oh, sure, dispose of the ogre. Is that all you want?"

The old nut didn't pick up on the sarcastic tone of my voice. He was thoroughly pleased by what he mistook as my acceptance of his ridiculous proposal. Nodding his head wildly, he flashed me another gross smile.

"You'll do it then!" he shouted excitedly.

"Like hell I will! You insane old rat! You're trying to get me to commit suicide. There's no way I'm going down there and fight that thing. It's an ogre. It's big, it's strong, and it's scary. But you should already know that, Mister I-know-all-about-ogres-and-you-don't. Also, did I mention before that it has a really big club?"

"Hold on. Just relax, you young hothead," the old sorcerer waved his hands back and forth, signaling for me to be quiet. "There's a way to defeat the creature without actually fighting it."

"Good, then you use it and let me know how everything turns out." I stood up and prepared to leave, this time for real. If this old loon thought he was going to go after the disc while the ogre was distracted chewing on my bones, he'd better think again.

The sorcerer rose from his chair with a loud grunt, and hobbled after me. "Now wait, Boy. Just wait a second. I told you," he said, panting from the exertion of having to stand, walk and speak all within the same hour, "ogres can't abide sunlight. It's not because they don't like it. Sunlight is death to them. They turn to brittle stone when touched by it."

I stopped in my tracks, turned, and looked at him. "So what, you want me to lure it into the sunlight? Is that it?"

The sorcerer nodded.

I thought about the sorcerer's idea for a moment. It wasn't without merit. If I were clever, I could get rid of the monster without coming to blows with it. Then assuming the old guy was right about the disc's power, this could be my chance to free myself of the curse. It was worth the risk.

"So if I get rid of the ogre for you, you'll use the disc to cure me, right?" I said, wanting to confirm our agreement.

"Not cure, stupid. I told you, the curse is too powerful. Even with the disc's magic, I can only remove a portion of it. I might be able to make it possible for you to remain human for two or three nights each month."

"Two or three nights? Is that all? That's the best you can do? How pathetic is that?" My hopes had been betrayed. I'd been counting on the entire curse being removed. What was the use of removing only a smidgen of it? Was that really going to make a difference in the way I could live?

"It's all that can be done," the sorcerer said, shrugging matter-of-factly. "So, what's it going to be, Boy?"

The kimch'i was in my pot now. It was up to me to either eat it or throw it out. What would I decide to do? The scheming old sorcerer waited for me to respond. He knew that he'd offered me something I couldn't refuse. I had little choice but to agree.

"I told you my name is Kang Goo-shu, you bony, deaf codger," I said, venting my frustration. I didn't like that I'd been manipulated into a corner. "Well, heck, any relief is better than none at all," I conceded halfheartedly.

The sorcerer grinned from one hairy ear to the other. "Good choice, Kang Goo-shu,"

I received a few final instructions before my departure. The old sorcerer laid out for me a means by which I might reach the lowest levels of the tower undetected by the ogre's super senses. First, however, I would require a few things from the alchemy lab. Because of the jammed doors, I'd have to do a little more climbing. I wasn't thrilled by this prospect, but if it meant I could avoid attracting the ogre's attention, I was game. I entrusted my duffel bag to the sorcerer but kept Wolf Whacker with me for defense and general peace of mind. Sliding it through the back of my sash, I left the observatory the same way I came — down the wall.

I made my way down to the library; then from there continued on to the alchemy lab. By the time I reached my destination, my aching fingers were again throbbing and red. I wished that I had some snow or cool water with which to soothe them. Trying my best to ignore the discomfort, I quietly approached the nearest window and looked inside. It was too dark to see much, but everything appeared calm. The bats were fast asleep in the rafters above and this time, I'd let them stay that way.

Slipping stealthily through the window, I went straight for the robes hanging near the door. Grabbing the nearest robe off the wall, I proceeded to the shelves that contained the chemicals, roots and powders. I'd noted before that many of the ingredients were strong smelling. I could use one of them to mask my own scent from the ogre.

Starting at the bottom of the nearest shelf, I opened up each jar. Taking a whiff of the contents, I compared the different smells. The jars all contained fairly neutral smelling powders. Next were the open dishes of roots and herbs. Most of these had strong, spicy smells that were rather pleasant. They wouldn't do at all. I wanted to repel the ogre, not make its mouth water. In the last dish on the shelf was a pair of thick, brown roots. Picking up one of the roots, I held it to my nose and took a sniff. I was assaulted by a bitter, rotten stench that bored through my sinuses and made my head spin. I couldn't push the thing

away fast enough. Keeping it at arm's length, I smiled as I wiped a tear from my watering eyes. I'd found my ogre repellent. Snapping the root in two, I discovered that the smell was even worse on the inside. A pale sap oozed from the broken ends. This was perfect. If I smeared this on the robe before I put it on, the ogre would never associate me with food.

Satisfied that I had what I needed, I placed the roots into the folds of my sash. I then tossed over my shoulder the robe that I'd taken. Returning to the window, I climbed out onto the eaves.

The next thing I had to do was return to the library. I tied the robe securely around my waist and started climbing. According to the old sorcerer, in the library I'd find a hidden passageway that I could use to get to the lower levels. The advantage of this route over the main stairs, which I could have accessed through the observatory door, was that it was safer. There was less chance of my being heard or smelled by the ogre, if I avoided the main staircase as much as possible.

When I at last reached the library level, I climbed through the nearest window and headed straight for the north wall. The sorcerer had said that, while searching for Mang-Wi artifacts, he'd discovered a secret passage behind the bookcase covering that section of the wall. This passage led from the library to a narrow, descending stairwell. The stairs ran directly under the main staircase and came out in the sleeping quarters on the third level. If I were lucky, once there, I could access the main stairs using the chamber door, and then continue down. The old sorcerer had provided me with an unattractive alternative if the bedchamber door were also jammed. There was a garbage chute that ran from the bedchamber to a catch bin at the base of the stairs on the bottom level. The sorcerer believed it large enough to fit me. It was my fervent hope that the chamber door opened. I loathed the idea of having to slide down some ancient sorcerer's nasty garbage hole.

Regardless of which route I ended up taking, I'd need to be careful. The ogre slept in a cave beneath the tower during the day. Moving about on the upper levels was probably safe, but the lower levels were another matter all together. The slightest noise or even the hint of a human scent could bring the creature down on me. Because the monster lived almost totally in darkness, its hearing and sense of smell were preternaturally acute. If I were detected, the sorcerer advised me to run for the nearest door or window and seek shelter in the daylight. The ogre wouldn't pursue me into direct sunlight.

The last thing that cowardly old fink said to me was not to bother running to him for help. He flat out stated that he wouldn't risk opening the observatory door for me. If I got into trouble, I was on my own.

Following the sorcerer's directions, I found the north wall bookcase. I then looked for the large leather-bound book he said would be on the middle shelf. Locating the book, I pulled on it as instructed. The book came out a ways then caught on something. From behind the wall I heard a loud, metallic "clack." A deep rumbling noise followed, accompanied by the clanking of heavy chains. Suddenly, the bookcase and a

section of the wall behind it began to slide outward. I stepped back and brought Wolf Whacker to the ready. If any hungry monsters came rushing out of that opening, I'd thwap them viciously (then run screaming in terror).

The bookcase slid out silently until it was perpendicular to the wall and then stopped. From the newly opened passage came a soft white glow that spilled into the library. Stepping closer, I looked inside. The stone-lined passageway defied my expectations. It wasn't dark and fore-

boding, as I'd envisioned. In fact, it was
brighter in the passageway than in the
library. This reassured me greatly and
I entered without trepidation.

The passage was twice the width
of my shoulders and a full arm's
length over my head in height.
Glowing stone orbs along the right
hand wall provided the curving passage with abundant light. The perfectly round, fist-sized stones were
evenly spaced at head level. Claw-shaped
holders, fastened to the wall, held them in
place.

Tentatively, I reached up and touched one of the
stones. It wasn't hot, as I had expected. Soft, white light was all it emit-
ted. This was amazing magic. The old sorcerer hadn't mentioned these.

Suspecting I'd find a use for such a stone later, I removed one from
its perch. The orb was lightweight and smooth. It felt very solid, not at
all flimsy or delicate. I wouldn't have to be paranoid about dropping it.

Delighted with my new discovery, I stuffed the stone into my now
bulging sash along with the stink roots. I removed the robe that I had
wrapped around my waist and tossed it over my shoulder for comfort
and ease of movement. Taking Wolf Whacker in a firm grip and holding it at the ready, I set off down the passageway.

The passage curved gradually following what I believed to be the
outer wall of the tower. It soon came to an abrupt end at a stone wall.
At the base of the wall was an opening in the floor. I looked closer and
saw that it was the entrance to a steep stairwell. More glow stones lit
the narrow, curving stairs as they descended into the tower.

I stepped through the opening and followed the stairs. The steps
were shallow, not even a full foot's length in depth. I had to walk
slightly sideways and keep one hand on the wall for balance.

"What kind of person would have found these stairs convenient?" I
asked myself.

The stairwell was cramped and utterly silent. At first, the abundance of light from the glow stones was a comfort against the hazardous conditions. I was glad not to be stumbling through the dark. However, as the minutes passed, the eeriness of my surroundings instilled in me an ever-growing sense of disquiet. I felt as though I were trespassing in someone's tomb. Did my uninvited presence here disturb the ghosts of the Mang-Wi? The curving nature of the stairs prevented me from seeing more than a half dozen paces ahead. This added to my growing dread of what I might encounter around the next bend. My imagination raced with thoughts of finding an angry specter waiting for me. Fortunately, aside from a few spiders and their pesky webs, nothing unpleasant greeted me as I made my way down the empty stairs.

The curvature of the stairs and the sharpness of their descent decreased the lower I went. Gradually, I was able to see farther and farther ahead. In addition, the steps became large enough for me to walk easily. This seemed to confirm my earlier assumption that the stairs ran along the tower's outer wall.

I'd gone down several hundred stairs, but there was no sign of a landing. I wondered what level I was on. I speculated that I was likely on, or near, level four. It amazed me to think that earlier in the day, I'd climbed this distance by hand. I'm such an unmatched stud!

On my next turn of the tower, I came upon an arched doorway built into the left-hand wall. Through it lay another well-lit corridor. The corridor led off to the left and curved out of sight. Strangely, the stairwell I was on didn't end here but continued to descend. This was puzzling. I knew that I'd come down quite a ways, but I didn't believe I'd come down far enough to have reached level three. Why didn't the stairs end here? The old sorcerer had said that they led from the library to the bedchamber. There was no mention of them opening onto another level or of them continuing on beyond that. Either the old coot had lied to me, or else he was even more senile than I thought. I wondered how much of what the old sorcerer had told me could be relied upon. Was all his talk about ogres not being able to tolerate sunlight inaccurate as well? And what if he couldn't use the disc to cure me as he'd promised?

I forced these doubts from my head. I had already come too far and endured too much to start second-guessing the outcome now. Come what may, I had to see this through to the end.

Poking my head through the doorway, I looked down the passage. More glow stones lined the right-hand side of the wall. What was down there? My curiosity was uncontrollable. While I was here, I told myself that I should at least investigate. Whether out of neglect or by intent, the old sorcerer had failed to mention this passage. It could mean that there was something important here.

Letting my curiosity take charge, I left the stairwell and followed the narrow corridor. I pushed my way through sheets of sticky cobwebs until I came to a heavy wooden door. The door at the end of the passage was almost identical to the others I'd seen in the tower. It was made from dark, aged wood with sturdy iron braces running horizontally across it. The major difference was that in the center of this door was embossed a large, golden emblem. It was a flaming circle: a golden wreath of fire. Within it were three dragon figures. The dragons were shown flying in a circle around a small gold disc.

Did this disc represent the one that the old sorcerer was after? Perhaps the disc was located behind this door? But that didn't make any sense. The old sorcerer knew of the secret passage and the stairway. He must have discovered this door as well. If the disc were behind it, why would he worry about the ogre? Since the monster didn't know about the secret doors and passages, it was safe to come down here. The old guy could have gotten the disc himself. Therefore, there had to be something important downstairs just as he'd said or else the ogre wouldn't be an issue. So what of this door? The little gold disc on the emblem pointed to a connection to the artifact that the sorcerer sought. My suspicions and curiosity intensified. The old man was definitely not being forthright with me.

I stepped closer and examined the door. There was no door ring, or handle, no obvious way of opening it. Thinking that it might open inward, I reached out to give it a push. Before I could even make contact, tiny bolts of blue lightning shot from the emblem and struck my outstretched hand. The shock staggered me and I jumped back, shuddering uncontrollably. For a moment I thought my knees might buckle and I leaned against the wall to brace myself. When my limbs stopped shaking, I grabbed my injured hand and rubbed it vigorously. The skin was numb and tingly. The little hairs on the back of my hand stood up like pine needles. I shook my hand in the air and opened and closed my fingers until normal feeling returned to them.

Someone had placed a wicked-nasty spell on the door, a darn painful one too.

Wary about getting too close, but not ready to give up, I decided to try again. This time I'd use Wolf Whacker in place of my hand. Taking a couple of steps back, I gripped the end of the staff and pushed it towards the door. Just as before, lightening erupted from the emblem. The energy had struck the tip of my staff before it could touch the door. Sizzling blue light danced and writhed across the end of the weapon, but didn't reach my hand. Ignoring the lightning, I pushed my staff against the door as hard as I could. The door didn't budge. I leaned into the effort with the full weight of my body, but to no avail. The door wasn't opening. Smoke began to rise from the end of Wolf Whacker. Not wanting my staff to burn, I quickly retracted it and used my foot to stamp out the black smoke coming from Wolf Whacker's tip.

From my failed endeavor, I learned that the door reacted whenever someone or something got close. I again asked the question, "What could be in there that was so valuable that it needed this kind of protection?"

There was no point in trying to use brute force to gain access. If the

ogre couldn't break down the doors in this tower, then I sure wouldn't fare any better. Only a magic user could get past that darn emblem.

With nothing to gain by staying any longer, I decided to leave the mystery of the magic door for later. I made a point to remember to ask the old sorcerer about it when this was all over.

Returning to the stairs, I continued to follow them down. It wasn't long before they bottomed out onto a small landing. The landing was connected to another narrow passageway. I was confident that this time I'd arrived at my intended destination. The distance I had come down felt right and the stairs ended here. This meant that the level with the magically sealed door was somewhere on the fourth level.

I brushed aside more cobwebs and followed this latest corridor until it dead-ended at the backside of another secret door. A pair of polished metal rods protruded from the right-hand wall. These connected to the top and bottom of the door like a set of outstretched arms. It wasn't difficult to figure out that these were a part of whatever mechanism opened the door. Hanging to one side of the door, was a thick rope that dangled through a hole in the ceiling. A heavy brass ball was tied to the end of the rope.

"Pull to open?" I whispered.

I gave the rope a firm tug.

From behind the wall to my right came the sounds of chains clanking and gears grinding together. The metal rods fastened to the door began to extend out from the wall, creaking as they pushed the door open. The chamber beyond the passage was dark. There were no glow stones in the room.

With Wolf Whacker at the ready, I stepped into the chamber. Without windows for ventilation, the air was stale. At least there would be no bats.

Needing light, I pulled the glow stone from my sash. Holding the orb up, its soft, white light brought immediate illumination. The bedchamber, as the old sorcerer had labeled it, was very spacious, but not lavishly decorated. There was a strange lack of furniture (namely a bed or sleeping mat). Its most noticeable features were the three enormous wood columns at its center. There were no carvings in the wood, only some simple decorations at their bases. Each column was connected at the top to a massive, circular wooden support that braced up the center of the ceiling. Extending from this central support out to the chamber wall were thick "v"-shaped crossbeams.

Strung between the columns were a series of heavy curtains. The curtains hung off the floor at waist level and extended up the columns a fair piece before slanting in sharply towards the middle. It was like looking at a giant tent, with the columns forming the poles by which the cloth sides were suspended. High above was a circular metal centerpiece that hung by ropes tied to the columns. The converging top ends of the curtains were brought together and secured to the centerpiece.

I knelt down and looked beneath the curtains to see what was behind them. What I saw was a circular, stone platform. The three great columns and draped curtains formed a triangular enclosure. I also observed that the curtain on the far side of the triangle was cut differently. The bottoms of the other two curtains ran at waist level from column to column. The curtain on the far side, however, was different. The bottom of that curtain arched up, creating an entryway into the center of the enclosed space.

Panning the glow stone around in a full circle, I gave the chamber a quick once-over to be sure I was alone. Confident that I was, I began to look about freely. I went first to the arched curtain. I wanted to examine the raised platform I'd seen within. Setting the burdensome robe on the floor a moment, I walked through the arched curtain, into the enclosed area. I discovered that what I had initially assumed to be simple curtains were in fact the backsides of huge tapestries. These tapestries were many times larger than those I'd seen in the observatory. In addition to the noticeable difference in size, their content was also dissimilar. These didn't tell a story, but instead drew upon nature for their theme. Depicted were wondrous scenes of unspoiled mountains, valleys and fields as green as any I'd ever seen in real life. There were lakes so calm that they reflected the sun and blue sky above with the clarity of crystals or polished metal. Wild deer drank from the glassy waters while butterflies flew lazily overhead. The grandeur of the tapestries wasn't due solely to their scope and realism but also to their exquisite detail. The depth of the pictures was stunning: from the delicate mottling on the animals' furs, to the rainbow-colored scales of the fish feeding in the shallow waters, to the tiny insects that rested on the blades of grass. And here again, there were dragons. The

mythical creatures were not as prominent here as they had been elsewhere in the tower. They were depicted only distantly, sitting majestically upon the pointed peaks of misty mountains, like shepherds watching over paradise.

Turning my attention away from the tapestries, I focused on the raised platform in the center of the floor. It was covered in fluffy pillows and brightly colored quilts. There was a noticeable layer of dust on all of the linen, but this didn't diminish the beautiful weaves of the fabrics.

I wondered, was this where the Mang-Wi slept? If so, their furnishings were a lot nicer than the old straw mats we had back in my village. The stone platform itself was small, not even long enough to lie down. This place must have been used for meditation rather than for sleeping. Perhaps the Mang-Wi didn't sleep at all. They may have simply meditated. That would make them very great beings. The teachers I'd had back in my village taught us the value of meditation as a means of focusing the mind and rejuvenating the spirit. Sleep, we were taught, was nature's crudest method of restoring life's energies, while meditation was the pinnacle. Through meditation, one communed with a consciousness that went beyond the physical. Those skilled in this art required only a few hours of sleep a day and always remained focused and alert. However, even the village masters who taught us these things could not completely replace sleep with meditation.

Leaving the enclosed area, I examined the rest of the chamber. It was fairly unremarkable. The only other items of any interest were four small, wooden chests resting against the wall near the chamber door. Walking over to the chests, I saw that they had been emptied and their contents, mostly clothing, tossed onto the floor. I suspected that this was the doing of the old sorcerer, probably during his search for Mang-Wi artifacts. If it had been the ogre, the entire chamber would've been smashed.

Finding nothing of interest amongst the contents of the chests, I decided it was time to leave. I retrieved the robe and slung it over my shoulder again. I then headed for the chamber door. It was bolted shut as the sorcerer had said it would be. The old man explained to me before I left, that he'd sealed what rooms he could as he fled to the observatory. This chamber had been the first. Afterwards, he'd made his way through the secret passage to the library. After bolting the library door, he then levitated down to the alchemy lab, sealed it, and then, floated up to the observatory. Wanting to save the library, I could understand, but it seemed like the old guy went to a lot of fuss just to safeguard a meditation chamber and a dusty old lab full of roots, pots and chemicals. No wonder he was still pooped.

Holding the glow stone to the door, I inspected its hinges. They looked intact, but the wood of the door showed signs of damage. Several planks were split lengthwise, attesting to the ogre's efforts to break through.

Quietly undoing the bolts, I pushed on the door. By the blessings of the gods, it opened. Finally, I thought, a door in this dump that actually worked. I wouldn't have to slide down the garbage chute after all. I quietly exited the bedchamber. The main staircase was just across a narrow, unlit landing.

Fearing that the light from my glow stone might attract the ogre, I partially concealed it within the folds of my sash. Glancing about, I wondered why there were no glow stones in the landing to provide light. There'd been none in any of the chambers I'd visited. Now to find the landings and stairs devoid of them as well was perplexing. The secret passage had an abundance of the glowing orbs. So what did the Mang-Wi use to see by when they weren't skulking around the tiny tunnels inside their walls?

I crept silently towards the stairs. As I did, I noticed that there were fixtures for glow stones along one side of the wall, or at least what was left of them. The claw-shaped holders for the stones had been smashed. Stepping nearer, I saw that the floor was littered with bits of shattered glow stone and the broken pieces of holders. The ogre had done this. The sorcerer said it lived almost totally in darkness. It was probably sensitive to the light of the orbs. I'd have to be careful about my own glow stone. The least little bit of light would likely be noticed. I slipped the stone all the way into my sash. The landing plunged into complete darkness. I groped my way along the wall towards the stairs. When I felt the drop-off of the first step, I eased the glow stone out of my sash just a tad. Seeing that the stairs were clear, I once more covered the stone's light. Quietly, I proceeded down the stairs. The slightest sound would travel a long way within these stone walls. Feeling my way through the darkness, I took each step one at a time and in deliberate fashion. My every breath was slow and measured, softer than a mouse's whisper.

Arriving at the second level landing, I paused and again brought out the glow stone. Its light showed the landing to be clear of danger. I also saw that the door on the other side was already partially open.

Keeping the glow stone out just enough to see, I crept towards the door. As I got closer, I noticed that the planks of the door were scratched and that one of the iron braces had been peeled back. The ogre! Instinctively, my grip on Wolf Whacker tightened. Despite the chill of the tower air, I found myself sweating. An icy trickle of perspiration ran down the back of my neck and caused me to shiver.

When I reached the door, I removed the glow stone fully from my sash and held it before me. I was far enough away from the stairs that I didn't need to worry about light filtering down to the chamber below. If the ogre happened to be in this room, I'd know soon enough.

Maintaining my distance, I used Wolf Whacker to open the door fully. The door swung out with an all-too-loud "creak." The shrill noise startled and angered me. I wanted to curse the door's stupid, old hinges for having betrayed my presence. I froze in place. Had the ogre heard the noise? Had I given myself away? I held my breath. My heart was pounding in my chest. My eyes darted from the open door back towards the stairs, waiting for the ogre to appear. After a long, tense silence, I began to relax. The monster hadn't heard, though how it could've missed it, I didn't

know. Nonetheless, I was grateful. I'd lucked out and that was all that mattered.

Holding the glow stone before me, I entered the chamber. The room was large, even larger than the bedchamber above. Shadowy piles of junk cluttered the floor. Some of the stuff had been stacked, but much of it lay in disorganized heaps. The chamber possessed no freestanding columns. Instead, white stone buttresses ran in sweeping arches up the sides of the wall.

Moving deeper into the cluttered space, I examined the items around me. There were numerous knocked over stacks of books, a couple of dusty old statues lying on their sides, some broken tiles and vases, a few pieces of smashed wood furniture and a lot of other things that I couldn't identify. Overall, the place was a mess. To my right, I noticed several tapestries lying in a rumpled pile on the floor. A few others remained partially hanging from the wall. They'd been badly torn. Huge diagonal claw marks had ruined the once beautifully woven images. I shook my head in sorrow. I loved the tapestries. It broke my heart to see any of them defaced. This was unmistakably the ogre's handiwork.

Upon closer observation, I realized that all of the objects around me were pieces of art of some form. Most were damaged or overturned.

Turning slowly to my left, I was startled by the sight of a massive figure standing only a few paces away. I let out an audible gasp and jumped back. I was about to swing Wolf Whacker at my attacker's head when my right foot landed on the rounded edge of a knocked over vase. This threw me off balance and I stumbled backwards. I tried to regain my footing by back peddling, but my legs caught on the edge of an open chest. I fell butt first into it. In the commotion, the glow stone dropped from my hand. Stuck in the chest, I hurried to establish some sort of defense. I thrust my staff outwards using a two-handed defensive grip and braced for my foe's attack. Meanwhile, the glow stone clinked and clanked across the floor. It came to a stop at the feet of the hovering figure. The glow stone's light was shining up at the unmoving form,

making it more clearly visible. I squinted and looked closer at it. I was mortified to see that what I'd mistaken for a menacing attacker was, in fact, nothing but a large statue. Carved from white stone, it had been fashioned in the semblance of a mighty warrior. The warrior wore an ornate suit of fine armor. In one hand, he held a long, curved sword. A shield resembling a winged dragon, rested against his leg.

"Merciful heavens," I sighed, relieved that this wasn't the ogre. My fear returned as I thought about all the noise I'd just made. My clumsy, clamorous stumbling had caused such a disturbance that even the old sorcerer upstairs must have heard it.

Picking myself up out of the chest, I ran to the statue and retrieved the glow stone. I quickly shoved it into the folds of my sash. I then moved behind the statue and ducked down to watch the chamber door. I was pretty certain the ogre wasn't already in the room, or I'd have been eaten by now.

In the darkness, my eyes strained to pick out any sign of movement, any hint that something was coming. I held my breath and listened. One minute passed and then two. There was still no sound of approaching footsteps, only silence. The pressure in my lungs was growing extremely uncomfortable. If the ogre were going to storm up here, it should've done so by now. I exhaled as silently as possible. Catching my breath, I pulled the glow stone from my tunic and stood. This was the second time that I'd made noise like a raging bull in a pottery shop and still the ogre hadn't come to investigate. The old sorcerer must have been wrong about how good its hearing was. Or else this ogre was deaf.

Stepping out from behind the statue, I looked up at it. "Stupid statue," I whispered angrily and gave it a light (but very quiet) kick in the ankle.

Upon closer inspection, I noticed something odd about the warrior. He seemed a little on the thin side. The armor was impressive, but the guy's physique wasn't the least bit muscular. He was actually rather scrawny. What I could see of the face wasn't very rugged or studly looking either. I held the glow stone up to the statue. I was shocked to discover that the warrior's face was that of a woman, a very young woman. This warrior was a girl!

This was new. I'd never heard of a warrior woman, much less a warrior girl. Usually, only glory-hungry noblemen and unfortunate peasants such as myself participated in stupid wars and battles — never women. Why would the Mang-Wi have a statue like this in their home? This was just another puzzle in a tower chocked full of mysteries, monsters and weird old men.

Figuring that by now there probably wasn't much daylight left, I decided to conclude my search. Tucking the glow stone into the folds of my sash, I returned to the landing, leaving the remainder of the chamber unexplored. Pressing my back against the wall, I crept in darkness towards the stairs. As I slid my feet across the floor, I could feel the broken pieces of glow stones and their holders. I maneuvered my feet carefully through the debris so as not to make any noise.

When I got to the edge of the stairs, I stopped. Before proceeding any further, I had to do something about my sweet, human smell. I dropped the robe I'd been carrying onto the floor. Reaching into my sash, I pulled out one of the broken root halves. I rubbed its stinky

juices onto the robe. The air quickly turned foul. When the first root half dried out, I discarded it and switched to the other. Once the juices of that one were exhausted, I snapped the remaining whole root in two and continued rubbing. By the time I finished, my eyes were watering profusely. The robe now gave off a powerful stench to rival even the worst underwear funk. Discarding the roots, I slipped on the reeking robe and pulled it tightly around my shoulders. I removed the glow stone from the folds of my sash just enough to see. Moving quietly down the stairs, I took short, shallow breaths. I didn't want the ogre to hear my breathing, but mainly, it was the only way I could tolerate the smell of the robe.

Once I reached the point where I could see down into the lower chamber, I stopped. Pulling the robe over my face, I crouched low. The robe covered all but my watering eyes.

Last night's fire had died out, leaving the main chamber almost completely dark. There was only a weak light coming from some-where along the left-hand wall. I crept down a few more stairs in an effort to identify the source. The light was coming from the gap through which the ogre had chased me the previous night. Faint sun-light was slipping in past the piles of rubble around the opening. The wall looked as if it had been badly torn up. The small hole that I remembered from last night was now much enlarged. The ogre had gone all-out trying to get at me.

The sunlight from the hole was barely enough to illuminate a small section of the chamber. I could just make out the faint outlines of a few of the pieces of tossed furniture. The dark shapes of the mas-sive dragon columns were also visible, but I could see none of their fine carvings. With a more comprehensive view of the room, I was able to count a total of six columns. They were arranged in two rows of three. Each row was set a good twenty paces apart. The columns obstructed much of my view. In spite of the sorcerer's assurances that the ogre would be in its cave at this time, I had to consider that the monster might be down there in the chamber, sleeping or lurking. There were just too many areas of darkness, too much I couldn't see.

I listened for any hint of the ogre's presence. If it were asleep, then maybe I could hear it snoring.

After several minutes of uneventful silence, I felt emboldened. I moved down another few steps. My new position allowed me to see farther into the chamber, but it was still so dark I couldn't make out details. I wasn't about to stroll brazenly down there without first knowing what was waiting for me. I decided to do something drastic.

Reaching into my sash, I removed the glow stone. I planned to roll it down the stairs and into the chamber. If the ogre were down there, the noise and light would draw the monster out and hopefully distract it long enough for me to get away. If the ogre didn't appear, then I was free to check out the chamber.

Positioning the glow stone in the center of the stairs, I gave it a gentle push. The stone rolled out from under the robe, clinking and clanking noisily. My muscles tensed with each clamorous tumble. I glanced nervously about, checking for movement. The ogre had to be hearing this racket. I fully expected the big, butt-ugly blue brute to come storming out of the shadows at any moment. I rose to the balls of my feet. I was prepared to make a swift getaway at the first sight of a horned head.

The glow stone hit the chamber floor and continued to roll into the room. It made it almost halfway across the chamber before being stopped by debris on the floor.

The glow stone's light revealed no visible dangers: only shadows and stillness. The chamber was apparently unoccupied. There were no sounds coming from the ogre's hole. Everything was quiet. In fact, things were a bit too quiet. Where was the monster? Its hearing was supposed to be superb. How could it not know that someone was stomping around up here? The absence of the ogre was no reason to complain, but I was left to wonder. Was the monster setting a trap for me? It might be trying to lure me closer before it pounced. The only way to find out would be to take a risk and go down there.

I wrapped the robe tightly about my shoulders and crept down the stairs. I could see the inky black maw of the ogre's hole off to my right. The old sorcerer said that the monster slept down there during the day. If that were true, then it was an awfully heavy sleeper.

I retrieved my glow stone and kept a wary eye on the black pit. The mere sight of it spooked me, but my curiosity drove me to investigate. I wanted to look inside and see what was down there. The ogre wasn't anywhere around. It was safe (probably).

Finally, fear gave way to impetuousness. Gritting my teeth, I walked towards the hole. As I did, I noticed a growing discomfort in my hands. I realized that I was clutching Wolf Whacker too tight. I had such a firm grip on it that the muscles in my hands had started to ache from the exertion. Halting in my tracks, I took a deep breath and forced myself to relax. A clear and focused mind was what I needed, not all this stiff tension. I took several more breaths and pushed aside thoughts of the ogre. My muscles began to relax and the rigidity eased out of them. I continued towards the pit. When I got to its edge, I held the glow stone over its black opening. Leaning slightly forward, I peered into it. The hole's darkness seemed to swallow the stone's light. I was barely able to see more than a few arms' lengths past the pit's edge. The bottom must have been deep in the earth. From somewhere in the blackness below I could hear the distant echo of water dripping on stone.

Stepping back from the edge, I shook my head. There was no way I'd ever go down there — not for anything. The vibes I was getting from just looking into the awful pit were too scary.

Leaving the hole behind, I set about having a look at the rest the chamber. Much of it I'd seen last night. Aside from the fire having died out, little had changed. The single notable exception was my little escape hole. The gap I'd crawled through last night was now much enlarged. Stepping closer, I saw that a significant section of the surrounding stone work had been gouged away. Entire blocks were broken and their jagged chunks shoved aside. The ogre's club and powerful hands had reduced the wall's thickness by half. I pulled away a few of the larger pieces of stone cluttering the opening. This allowed in more sunlight. Getting down on my hands and knees, I reached through the opening and touched the grass growing along the outside of the tower wall.

The ogre's strength was frightening. If the brutish freak ever got its hands on me, I'd be a goner. I'd need to think up an ingenious, surefire plan. My goal was to introduce that monster to its first and last killer suntan and live to tell about it. There were only two possible sources of sunlight that I could see. The first was the hole in the wall. The second was the main door, which lay at the other end of the chamber. The hole wouldn't be of much use. It was way too small. The ogre would never fit all the way through it. The door on the other hand, was more than large enough. However, I doubted whether even the ogre would be stupid enough to follow me out into the daylight. I'd have to find a way to bring sunlight to the monster.

I headed for the main door. Along the way, I had to step over the scattered pieces of broken cooking pottery, dishes and furniture. The floor was littered with things that the ogre had destroyed. When I got close enough to see, I noticed that the door's dead bolts were locked. Its wooden planks and hinges remained undamaged. The ogre, apparently, hadn't even tried to open it. Pulling back on the dead bolts, I unlocked the door and gave the opening ring a hard tug. The door opened, but not easily. It was extremely heavy. At least it was quieter than the door upstairs. Opening the door fully, I looked outside. The trees that bordered the clearing were a short distance away. Beyond the trees, I could see the low ranges of eastern hills. Their rounded peaks were awash in the waning light of the setting sun.

Out of this tranquil image sprung to my mind an idea of unparalleled brilliance. Running back inside, I again looked over the layout of the chamber. The ogre's hole was directly in line with the door. The fireplace was but a short distance beyond that. When the sun rose tomorrow morning, it would come up over the hills facing the door. If the door were open, the light would pour in, hitting the hole and the fireplace. The fireplace, with all of its reflective tiles, would catch the sunlight and flood the entire chamber with light. The dragon columns were well off to the sides and would block none of the light. The ogre wouldn't stand a chance if it were anywhere near the center of the room.

The plan was perfect. All I had to do was keep the monster in the chamber and in line with the door. When I opened the door at sunrise, the ogre would roast like a chestnut. The timing would be crucial, but I was confident that I could make it work.

"I'm such a genius," I proclaimed out loud.

That grouchy goat of a sorcerer had called me a dumb farm boy. Could a dumb farm boy come up with such a brilliant plan, you

wrinkly old wart?

With sunset nearing, I worked quickly. I propped the door open enough so that I might detect from the stairs the sun rising over the hills. Hurrying back up the stairs, I took up a position at the point where the stairs met the ceiling. This left me a narrow view of the lower chamber. From here, the ogre's hole and the door were visible. If everything went well, I'd remain in this spot until sunrise. I'd only need to move from here if the ogre came near me, or if it attempted to go back down its hole. Should the beast try to leave before sunrise, I'd have to do something to stop it. At the moment, however, I had no idea what that something might be. I'd cross that bridge when I came to it.

In the meantime, my transformation into a chicken was moments away and I had to prepare. I could already feel its onset. I removed my clothing and piled them beside Wolf Whacker on the stairs next to me. I kept these things concealed beneath the cover of the robe, since they carried my scent. As for the glow stone, I placed it close beside me so that I wouldn't have to sit out the night in total darkness.

I pulled the robe completely over me and crouched down low on the stairs. Giving a long-suffering sigh, I settled in to wait. A minute later the transformation occurred and I was once more a miserable little chicken. Covering the glow stone with one wing, I wriggled my beaked face out from under the robe.

Where was the ogre? It was after sunset. Shouldn't it be here by now?

Hours passed with no sign of the beast. I began to wonder if perhaps it had decided to move on and find some other place to ransack.

As the night wore on, the tower's normally chill air got just plain cold. At times like this, I appreciated having feathers. It was like wearing a down blanket. More hours passed and I continued to wait. I thought that I would go mad from the unrelenting boredom. The quiet and endless stillness made the temptation to sleep unbearable. I fought the urge to doze off for even just a few moments. I had to stay alert. I took to staring into the soft, white light of the glow stone to help keep me awake.

As the night continued to drag on, my hunger became more acute. Having eaten only a few roasted chestnuts all day, I was starving. The pangs were so bad that even the thought of wolfing down an icky worm or slime-oozing grub no longer grossed me out. I wished that one of those chubby spiders I had seen in the secret passage would come crawling along. To my disappointment, none did. I went hungry. Eventually, I took to playing games of tic-tac-toe to distract myself. Using the light of the glow stone to see by, I scratched the "x"s and "o"s into the stairs with my talons. By the one hundred and fifth game, my interest and concentra-

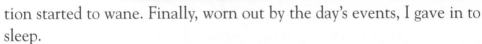

tion started to wane. Finally, worn out by the day's events, I gave in to sleep.

When I awoke, it was with a frightened start. From the chamber below, I heard a harsh, scraping noise. It was distant and irregular. My heart began to race. I peeked out from under the robe and stared wide-eyed into the dark-ness. I could see absolutely noth-

ing at first. Before long I began to notice a faint blue glow outlining the rim of the ogre's pit. I thought my tired eyes were playing tricks on me. I rubbed at them with my wing, but the glow remained. I watched, as it grew steadily brighter. As the source of the light came closer, the

scraping sounds got louder. It sounded like something hard and sharp was scratching against rock.

Claws?

The ogre was coming!

My skinny legs began to shake with fear. It was a struggle to keep my knees from knocking against one another and making noise. Transfixed, I watched with unblinking eyes.

The ogre's hands and arms emerged from the pit proceeded by the blue glow. I saw now that it was the ogre's skin that was the source of the light. The glow it produced was subtle but striking. It was enough to make the monster and a small area around it, eerily visible.

The old sorcerer hadn't mentioned anything about ogres glowing in the dark. It hadn't been glowing the last time I saw it. Perhaps this effect only occurred when the beast was in total darkness?

The ogre lumbered away from the hole and headed for the fireplace. Over one of its shoulders the brute carried its massive bone club. There were deep cracks and chips in it that hadn't been there before. The tower wall had taken a heavy toll on the weapon. The old bone didn't look like it would hold together much longer. In the ogre's other hand it dragged something large. I squinted harder to bring the object into focus. It was a mountain buck. The ogre was dragging the lifeless animal by its antlers across the floor.

So this was why the monster hadn't shown up until now; it had been off hunting. It was bringing its food back here to eat.

The ogre walked past the fireplace towards the table I had seen earlier and disappeared from sight. Only a single corner of the wooden table was visible from my vantage point. I waited and listened for a clue as to what the ogre might be doing. An instant later I heard a meaty thud and saw the table shudder. The ogre must have thrown the deer carcass onto the table. Soon a barrage of horrible munching and slurping sounds assaulted my ears. The sounds were disgustingly vivid. I ducked under the robe and covered my head with my wings to drown out the awful racket. It was to no avail. The slobbering, chomping and belching were too loud to be ignored.

As the ogre's meal dragged on, I began to feel nauseous. Any desire I'd had for food was squelched by the monster's grotesque feeding noises.

After about an hour, the ghastly feast ended. I could still hear the ogre's breathing, but it wasn't moving around.

Peeking out from under the robe, I took a look. I couldn't see the ogre, just the glow from its body. It was resting somewhere near the fireplace. Suddenly, there was a loud, thunderous belch, followed immediately by a contented sigh.

The ogre had crudely confirmed for me its location. The brute had apparently settled down for a nice snooze. I just hoped it would stay put until sunrise. Glancing towards the door, I could see the pale yellow/orange light of the pre-dawn sun. It wouldn't be long until the first rays of morning light appeared through the crack of the open door. When that happened, I could make my move.

Within minutes, the ogre was snoring loudly. It was fast asleep.

"Perfect!" I thought to myself. Now the monster wouldn't be going anywhere, I just had to be patient and wait.

As the final hour before dawn passed, the ogre's snoring continued. I struggled against my own desire to sleep. Repeatedly, I stifled my drowsy yawns for fear that they'd awaken the nasty creature prematurely.

Just as I felt myself starting to nod off again, there was an unexpected explosion. The noise had come from the direction of the fireplace. It took me a moment to realize what it was I'd just heard. It was a fart, a great monster of an ogre fart. In fact, it was the loudest, bunghole-ripper I'd ever heard. The blast was of such volume and force I feared it might topple the chamber columns and shake loose the ceiling beams.

I was aghast. How could a creature, even one as disgusting as the ogre, cut loose such an evil thing?

There wasn't time to think further on this foulness. The ogre awoke with a startled growl. The sick, silly brute had roused itself with its own flatulence. If it were not for the timing, the situation would've been laughable. However, it was too soon for the ogre to wake up. It was still some minutes before sunrise. If the monster decided to meander back down its hole, my plan would be in jeopardy.

As fate would have it, that was precisely what the ogre started to do. I heard it grunt and yawn as it staggered back to its feet. Dragging its club along the floor, the creature lumbered sleepily into view. It was still tired, not totally alert. Nevertheless, the brute was headed straight for its hole.

This was bad.

What could I do to keep the monster here? There was only one sure way.

Crawling slightly out from under the robe, I waved one wing back and forth, wafting my chicken scent at the ogre.

The monster reached the edge of the pit but suddenly stopped. The ogre raised its head and sniffed at the air. It growled low and menacingly. The brute had caught my scent.

I ducked back under the robe so its stink would once more conceal me. With any luck, the ogre would remain interested and linger a while longer.

I lifted the edge of the robe enough to see. The ogre turned its head, this way and that, trying to locate the source of the odor it had detected. It took in great drafts of air as it sniffed. The monster growled again. It had definitely caught wind of me. The noises it made became more eager, more intense.

"Liked what you smelled, huh? Well, stick around you toad-kissing crud. I've got more than just the scent of wholesome-poultry-goodness in store for you," I thought to myself. I was excited. In a few minutes, I'd be able to spring my trap.

The ogre sniffed the air again and snorted. Then, oddly, it seemed to lose interest. Giving a listless shrug, it started to enter the hole.

I obviously hadn't given the ogre enough of a whiff. There was no time left for subtlety or half-measures. I quickly turned and stuck my bottom out from under the robe. I began waving my feathered fanny vigorously to and fro.

Immediately, the ogre stopped. It climbed back out of the hole, snorting. The vile creature turned to look in my direction. I was barely able to get my bottom back under cover before being spotted.

I peeked out from under the edge of the robe. The ogre's ugly mug was facing in my direction. The beast grunted softly and growled. As the creature continued to sample the air, the primal sounds turned angry and got louder. The beast brought its club down off its shoulder and held it in two hands. Cocking its head to the side, the monster sniffed the air, searching for the origin of the smell. The blue glow of its skin made its hideous face appear even more monstrous. Just when I thought that the ogre couldn't look any uglier, out came its tongue. Long and black, the forked tongue lapped at the air, sampling it. The creature's lips curled into a frightening snarl. Thick, dark drool dripped from its tusk-like teeth. Its eyes fixed on my location and narrowed into sinister slits. Suddenly, the beast let loose a horrific roar. It started stomping towards the staircase. Each stride it took was like a mighty hammer pounding on the tiled floor. I could feel the vibrations even from on the stairs.

Uh-oh! I'd given the ogre too much of a whiff. It knew exactly where I was.

I didn't know what to do. Should I make a run for the secret passage or remain where I was and hope for the best. Maybe the ogre didn't know for certain where I was. This moment of indecision eliminated the first option. The ogre covered the distance to the stairs with only a few giant strides. It stood alongside the staircase, its toothy maw only a wing's length away from the edge of the robe.

I lay as flat against the stairs as I could, wishing that I could just melt into the stone and disappear.

The ogre poked its nose closer and sniffed at the edge of the robe. It immediately jerked its head back and hacked.

The stinky robe worked. My sacrifice in having to suffer its smell all these hours hadn't been in vain.

The stubborn crea-ture brought its face in closer to the robe a second time. Its yellow eyes gleamed bright and angry.

I used my wings to com-pletely cover the glow stone's light.

The ogre g r o w l e d

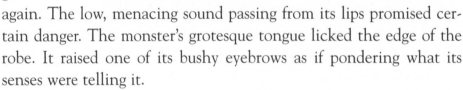

again. The low, menacing sound passing from its lips promised cer-tain danger. The monster's grotesque tongue licked the edge of the robe. It raised one of its bushy eyebrows as if pondering what its senses were telling it.

Without warning, the ogre let out a horrifying roar that vibrated throughout the chamber. My poor, traumatized heart skipped at least a beat or two as a result. The ogre raised its club high. The brute was going to flatten the robe (and me).

Without thinking, I pushed the glow stone out from under the robe. It rolled over the side of the staircase and fell at the ogre's feet.

Blinded by the brightness of the orb's light, the ogre halted its attack in mid-strike and covered its eyes with both of its arms.

Taking advantage of the distraction, I leaped from beneath the robe and jumped past the ogre's head. With my inadequately small wings flapping madly, I did my best to fly. I managed only a short dis-tance before gravity pulled me down.

The ogre was angered by my trick and the pain caused by the glow stone's light. Enraged, the monster swung about and raised its club high. The beast bellowed furiously and charged after me.

With dawn only moments away, I could feel the transformation coming. I needed to reach the door

and get outside. The door was cracked open enough that I could fit through. If I were lucky, the ogre would follow me out into the sun.

I was running for the door as fast as I could. Behind me, I could hear the pounding of the ogre's big, blue mud flaps. All of a sudden, a huge white blur swooshed over my head. The object crashed noisily to the floor in front of me. It was the ogre's club. The monster had tossed its weapon at me, barely missing my head. I jumped back to avoid plowing into the giant bone.

Glancing back, I saw the ogre was almost on top of me. I scurried to my left just as it dove at me. Its huge, blue body hit the floor with such force that it bounced me off my feet entirely. While on its belly, the monster reached out to snatch a hold of me. Before it could, I flapped my wings and jumped up, avoiding danger. The instant I landed, I took off running. However, in my haste, I'd bolted in the wrong direction. I was running back towards the ogre's pit and the fireplace.

The ogre had also gotten to its feet. It now stood between me and the door.

This was not good.

I stopped and glanced wildly about, searching for some way around the monster. Before I could formulate a plan, the ogre charged at me again. I had no choice but to run straight ahead, in the opposite direction of the door. Still, I wanted to avoid going anywhere near the ogre's pit. I veered slightly to the right and headed for the table. I hoped to use it as an obstacle. If I hid under it, it might force the ogre to circle to one side. This would clear a way for me back to the door.

I reached the table and heard another thunderous roar. Looking back, my terrified eyes beheld a huge heap of blue blubber diving straight at me. Sheer panic energized me. I dashed forward and scurried under the table just as the ogre belly-flopped on the floor. Its arms and hands thrashed and swiped at me, but I was too fast. I got away and ran out the far end of the table. The ogre was still on the ground as I turned back and faced the door. This was my opportunity.

Flapping my wings, I jumped atop the table. Its other end faced in the direction of the door. Rather than going around the dumb monster, I'd go over it. I sprinted across the tabletop toward the other end intent on hopping on the ogre's back and making a beeline for the door. I hadn't gotten even half way when the ogre sprang to its knees. The monster glared at me with hate. It roared furiously and lashed out, hammering on the end of the table with both its fists. The table legs on that end gave out and the tabletop splintered and shattered.

The next instant was a jumbled blur as the whole table upended. I felt my little body being shot into the air. I was hurled right over the ogre's head. My confusion turned to elation as I realized that the stupid monster had inadvertently helped me. By the time my feet touched the ground again I was half way to the door. Running for my feathered life, I hurried to cover the remaining distance. The door was just ahead. I could see the first rays of the sun shinning through its opening. I was sure that I'd make it out this time, when suddenly, a dark shadow passed overhead. I watched in disbelief as the wooden table flew past me and crashed sideways into the door. The impact slammed the door shut, sealing me in the room.

I was again forced to come to a screeching halt (only this time I didn't quite make it). My speed was too great and I ended up crashing beak first into the broken table.

I shook the stars from my head. I couldn't believe how fortunate I was. For the second time, the ogre had overshot while throwing a heavy object at me. The down side was that the table's impact had

ended any chance of me getting through the door, at least until I transformed. Without my human body, I couldn't move the table and get out. I was stuck in here, trapped with that monster.

From behind me there came the pounding of heavy feet running and angry snorts. There wasn't time to wait for my transformation. I looked back. The ogre was bearing down on me. I needed another way out. The hole in the wall! It dawned on me that I could get out through it. It was closer than the stairs and led out into the sunlight.

The onrushing ogre blocked my direct path to the hole, but I was tired of avoiding the brute. I charged straight at it. Surprised that I was no longer running away from it, the ogre was slow to react. Too late, it bent down and tried to scoop me up. At the last instant, I surprised the ogre again by bolting suddenly to the left. The monster's flailing hands just missed me. It spun to the side, following my movement and tried a second time to grab me. Once again I turned quickly, this time running back in the other direction. My incredible speed and agility confounded the dumb brute. It tried to keep up with me, but instead almost tripped itself. With the ogre off balance, I seized the moment and ran straight between its legs. Before the monster could turn

around, I was behind it and gone. I scurried around one of the dragon columns and headed straight for the gap in the wall.

My tiny, feathered body may not have been built for speedy, long distance running, but in tight spaces I was mind-bogglingly fast. The ogre couldn't catch me. I was slicker than snail snot. Utilizing the lead I'd gained, I hopped over the rocks and loose stones at the opening of the hole and crawled inside. Safety was only seconds away. My feathered shoulders scraped against the sides of the gap. At last, I squeezed through the other end of the opening and stood outside. I had made it. I inhaled and took in a breath of non-ogre fetid air. I could feel the change to human coming.

All of a sudden, a massive hand grabbed me from behind. The ogre had reached through the expanded gap and now held me in an unbreakable grip. I'd been such a fool to stop so close to the opening. Now I was going to pay for that mistake with my life. The muscular hand was rapidly squeezing the life from me. The ogre tried to pull me back inside, but I resisted with all my might. My outstretched chicken-

toes clung tenaciously to the edges of the opening. I poured my heart into the struggle, but chicken strength alone was useless. What saved me was the fact that the ogre's closed fist was too big. As long as it was balled up, it would never fit back through the narrow opening on this side. Refusing to release its prize, the ogre was like a monkey with its hand caught in a gourd. It was stuck. I found little victory in this, however, as the brute's stubbornness was crushing me. My eyes were bulging in their sockets from the increasing pressure. I was going to be squished like a ripe plum. The warmth of the morning sun now shining on my beak would be the last thing I'd feel.

"The sun!" I heard myself gasp in actual words. It was sunrise; the transformation had already started. As my body struggled to expand within the ogre's grip, I heard from behind me an awful wail. Smoke was rising from the ogre's hand. The monster shrieked in pain and as it did, it released me. In that same instant, I returned to full human form and collapsed on the ground. Looking back, I caught sight of the ogre's blackened, smoking hand as it disappeared back through the opening.

Gasping for air, I rubbed my aching ribs and neck. Another second or two and I'd have been finished.

"Speaking of finished," I said out loud. I still had something to do and I was looking forward to doing it.

Getting to my feet, I ran around the side of the tower to the door. When I got to it, I gave it a hard kick and flung it wide open. The table that was blocking it from the other side went crashing across the floor.

At the far end of the chamber, I saw the ogre. It was making its way towards the safety of its pit. My noisy entrance stopped the beast in its tracks. It stood in the center of the room, glaring at me with its yellow eyes. I remained in the doorway glaring back. The monster was cradling its right hand protectively. The brief exposure to sunlight had burnt it black. For a moment, while we traded dirty looks, the dumb beast was indecisive, uncertain whether to continue for its hole, or to attack. I didn't give it a chance to make up its mind.

Stepping clear of the doorway, I allowed the sun's rays to shine through. The sunlight struck the ogre and the fireplace behind it. The monster let out a hideous bellow. It shrieked in pain as its skin crackled and burned. Simultaneously, amplified sunlight bounced off of the fireplace's reflective tiles and struck the ogre from behind. Smoke billowed from the creature's body in great, dark plumes. The ogre was doomed. Its screams echoed throughout the chamber.

I became sick from the awful sounds and clasped my hands over my ears. Turning away in revulsion, I prayed for the shrieking to stop. Within seconds it did, with frightening abruptness. The only sound left

was a sickening crackling noise, the kind that burning wood makes. Dark smoke rolled listlessly throughout the chamber, making it impossible to tell what had become of the ogre. I waited a few minutes for the smoke to clear. When it had done so enough that I could see, I entered. Greasy black clouds lingered overhead as I made my way towards the back of the room. An awful sulfur smell pervaded the air and grew stronger the farther in I went.

Was this what cooked ogre smelled like? It was nasty. It would never become a delicacy.

By the time I neared the center of the chamber, I could see the dark shape of the ogre a short distance ahead. It stood motionless, like a statue. Moving closer, I saw that the creature's body had changed. It was now gray and powdery. It looked like ash. Its pose captured the terrible pain it had suffered in its final moments. Both of the ogre's arms were raised in an effort to fend off the rays of the sun. The creature's massive body twisted back, its face frozen in a final, ghastly wail.

Inching forward, I tentatively touched the powdery surface. I had no sooner done so, when without warning, the ogre's legs crumbled out from beneath it. Unsupported, the body toppled to the floor and burst apart in a spectacular eruption of ash and charred chips.

Fanning away the clouds of ogre dust, I went to the base of the stairs and picked up my glow stone. I returned to where I had left my clothes and staff. After dressing, I tossed the smelly robe over the railing of the stairs. The farther away it was from my nose, the better. With Wolf Whacker in hand, I headed upstairs. There was an old sorcerer at the top of this tower who owed me some relief from my curse. I was eager to claim my due. After what I had been through, I'd earned it.

Using the main staircase, I made my way to the observatory. It was a long, hard climb even with the convenience of stairs. As I passed through the various landings on each level, I saw what damage the ogre had done. The doors, that the old sorcerer had locked, remained shut. Their outsides bore the scars of the ogre's violent attempts to gain entrance. Those chambers that hadn't been sealed lay open and ransacked.

Reaching the top landing, I pounded on the observatory door.

"Hey, Old Man, the ogre's dead. You can stop hiding behind the tapestries and come out now," I shouted.

"The beast has been turned to stone then?" the sorcerer inquired from behind the closed door.

"Well, actually, it just kind of went 'poof,' but trust me, that's just as good. It won't be bothering you any more," I announced. "That is, unless you're allergic to dust," I said mumbling to myself.

"Excellent! Well done," the sorcerer said, sounding pleased. Through the door I could hear him cackling dryly. A moment later, the old guy began grunting and groaning. He began to pull the furniture away from the door. The wheezing and grunting sounds the old man made as he strained to clear the barricade were easily heard, even through the thick wooden door. Then, abruptly, the noise ceased.

"Boy," the old sorcerer called out again, "I was thinking."

"The name is Goo-shu, not Boy, you old wart. What's the delay? Just open the door." I wasn't in the mood for games. I was hungry and tired and my ribs and neck hurt from the ogre having squeezed the puss out of me. All I wanted was for my curse to be (partially) removed so that I could leave this place.

The sorcerer ignored me and continued on with what he wanted to say. "While you were in the dining chamber, did you by chance notice a large wooden chest?"

The old man had to be referring to the chest I'd seen the ogre poking through the night before last. "Yes, what of it?" I replied impatiently.

"Be a good lad and see if you can open it for me."

"There's no need. The ogre's already done that for you."

"Good. That's perfect," the old man said. He sounded thoroughly pleased to hear this news. "Then please fetch for me the gold disc. You'll find it in a black box within the chest."

That the old sorcerer had actually bothered to say "please" put me on my guard. He wasn't this polite by nature. He was simply too lazy to walk down all those stairs and fetch it himself. He wanted me to do it for him. I'd just climbed up here and I wasn't anxious to turn around and make another round trip. All that huffing and puffing aggravated my sore ribs.

"What's wrong with you going down there and getting it while I wait up here and have a rest? I've had a boogerishly long night," I complained.

"Go on. Get! You lazy, oafish lout," the sorcerer yelled, discarding any pretense of civility. "You should be back by the time I'm done moving this furniture."

I shook my head and sighed plaintively. It probably would take that rickety old codger that long to clear the door anyway. I might as well use the time productively and do as he'd asked. "Fine! Fine already! I'll be right back," I said, giving in. "But don't you croak before you get that door unlocked."

I returned to the first level and searched the chest for the black box that the sorcerer wanted. The ogre had smashed most of the chest's contents. All I found was broken junk. There was no sign of a black box. Then I remembered. There had been a black box in the chest. It was shiny and heavy looking. The ogre had found the box, sniffed it, and then tossed it aside. But where was it now? I thought back to the other night, trying to remember the direction in which the box had been thrown.

The stairs! The ogre had tossed the box towards the stairs. I rushed to the base of the stairs and began looking. A glint of gold immediately caught my eye. Looking for the source, I spotted the box. A small gold decoration on one side of the box had reflected the light. The box lay at the side of the stairs amongst the remnants of several shattered clay jars. Despite the rough way in which the ogre had discarded the box, it appeared undamaged and unopened.

I picked up the box and was immediately surprised at how heavy it was. It felt as if I were holding a block of solid rock. The box's surface was smooth, like a stone from a stream or river. Turning the box over, I inspected it thoroughly. Its length and width were slightly greater than that of my open hand, but its height was less than half that. There wasn't a single latch on it anywhere. In fact, as far as I could tell, there weren't even any hinges. There was also no seam to indicate where it might open. Shaking the box, I felt something shift inside. It was definitely hollow, but how did I go about opening it? Except for the embossing of a small gold dragon on one side, the box's surface was completely plain.

"Well, this has to be of significance," I said to myself.

With nothing to lose, I gave the emblem a push. It felt solid and didn't recess like a button or shift like a latch. It was just a decoration. I removed my finger from the emblem only to see it shimmer and then dissolve like a golden vapor. Suddenly, a glowing seam materialized along the sides of the box, partitioning it into top and bottom halves. As the two halves popped apart, there was a brief hiss of escaping air.

I separated the halves and looked inside the box. What I found was a magnificent disc of solid gold. It was slightly larger than my fist and had gently rounded edges. Discarding the lid of the box, I marveled at the brilliant object. The disc's mirrored surface seemed to glow with an inner light. I'd never seen anything so beautiful. It was elegant in its simplicity. There were no markings or writing spoiling its unblemished surface. When I ran my fingers over it, I was surprised to feel a strange, indescribable power pulsating from within it. I felt a charge enter through my fingers and course up my arm and into my body. The sensation wasn't unpleasant as the shock from the magic door had been. This was rather soothing.

Intrigued by the effects of my limited contact with the disc, I set my hand flat upon it. The sensation intensified. It was invigorating, energizing, a total rush. My weariness faded instantly. The thirst and hunger that had gnawed at me disappeared. Even the pain in my neck and sides was gone. I felt more energetic than I'd ever been in my life. I could understand why the old sorcerer would want to find this object;

just touching it was beyond cool.

Discarding the lower half of the case, I slipped the disc into my sash and headed back upstairs. The door to the observatory was already open by the time I got there. The old sorcerer stood waiting anxiously in the doorway.

"Were you able to open the box? Do you have it? Do you have the disc?" he asked, desperate for my answer. His hands trembled nervously at his sides.

I reached into my sash and brought forth the gold disc.

The sorcerer stumbled forward and snatched it from my hand, letting out a childlike giggle. I'm ashamed to say it, but it actually gave me the creeps to see him so happy.

The old man's eyes were wide as he cradled the disc in his hands. "Its design is much simpler than I'd imagined. It's smaller too," he said, sounding disappointed.

"It's solid gold, you dissatisfied old coot. What more could you want?" I grumbled under my breath.

Paying no heed to me, the old sorcerer continued to stare at the disc, turning it over in his hands. Closing his eyes, he pressed his palms tightly down on it and took a deep breath. He broke into a broad smile as he reacted to the disc's energy. The old man's posture straightened and I could see the tension ease from his face.

After a few moments he again opened his eyes and spoke, "Do you know how long I've searched for this? Do you?" he asked.

"If I say 'yes,' do you still have to tell me?" I sighed.

"Sixty-nine years, Boy. For sixty-nine long, arduous years have I searched. The incantations and spells I've learned are worthless without pure, mystical power. Power such as what is contained within this object." The sorcerer held the disc up and inspected it in the candlelight. As he turned it slowly over in his hands, the disc's reflective surface caught the firelight and sent sparkling flickers across the chamber. The old sorcerer continued to stare unblinkingly into the disc. It made me more than a little nervous. I wanted him to hurry up and remove the curse from me so that I could get away from him. The kooky vibes he was giving off were disturbing.

"For millennia it has been sought after by magi and adventurers. Now it's mine. Through this, I'll be able to perform the old magics as they were meant to be, and you shall watch me. Marvel, Boy, marvel and be amazed. Not since the heavens were last cracked open has this disc's energies been unleashed."

The old sorcerer paused to catch his breath. His ranting had tired him out. He looked peaked.

"Guys have been looking for it for millennia, huh? Wow! And you've been after it for sixty-nine years? That's a long time. You do know, of course, that it only took me two minutes to find the thing. I guess you must've been doing something wrong all those years," I joked.

"Don't mistake a fool's luck for scholarly skill and dedication, you tiresome pup," the sorcerer rebuked. "Being so young, you do not yet appreciate the passage of years or what it means to spend your life in pursuit of a dream."

"But you're wrong, Sir. I do know what it means to pursue a dream. I came here looking for a way to rid myself of my curse and you promised to help me with that. Now, before you waste another sixty-nine years talking my ear off, how about making good on your promise and doing what you can for me?"

At first the sorcerer sneered resentfully at my impatience. I thought he was about to say something nasty. Instead, his expression softened and he nodded his acquiescence. Turning, he walked to the table at the other end of the chamber. I followed him. On the table was an old scroll. Its ends were tattered and frayed with age. Weights had been placed on the ends to keep it open. Looking closer at the scroll, I noted the writing on it. It was the same as that on the tapestries and in the books in the library.

The sorcerer bent forward and examined the scroll for a moment. He then mumbled a few indecipherable words to himself. Straightening up, he turned to me. Holding the gold disc in both hands, he closed his eyes. The sorcerer raised the disc over his head and began to chant in a strange, guttural language. Within moments, a gentle hum filled the entire chamber. I couldn't identify the source of the sound. It seemed to come from all directions. Slowly, the disc began to glow with a wondrous golden light. The old sorcerer was as motionless as a statue as the light washed over him. In seconds, his body was totally engulfed.

When I thought I saw the old man's skin beginning to glow, I figured for sure that I was hallucinating. I rubbed my eyes, but what I saw didn't change. The old man's skin was definitely aglow and it was getting brighter. The sorcerer's hunched posture straightened until he stood fully upright. His scrawny-bone-sack of a body filled out, giving him a healthier appearance.

I was speechless as I watched the transformation.

Gradually, the golden light faded. It receded back into the disc and the hum died down with it until there was again silence.

Finding my voice, I stammered, "Are…are you okay?" Given the appearance of the old man, I felt rather foolish for asking the question. He looked stronger than ever. His face had changed greatly. Before it had resembled crumpled paper, bumpy and full of wrinkles. Now the lines of age were diminished. He looked a good ten years younger and far peppier. Of course, the black eyesore of a wart on his chin remained. That was too bad. I'd have been happy if that had disappeared.

"I haven't felt this good in years," the sorcerer said. His voice was also different. It was softer, more considerate, almost charming.

Up until this point, I'd believed that I held a monopoly on strange transformations, but this was bizarre enough to challenge that claim. The disc's power had revitalized the sorcerer and reversed some of his age. He was still pretty old looking, but no longer ancient in appearance. Even the old guy's manner and temperament were improved. There was a gentle quality to him that had previously been totally lacking. It was a new man that stood in front of me.

The sorcerer smiled at me. "Now, for you, Lad. As per our agreement, I shall remove from you what portion of the curse I can."

Setting his cane beside the table, the sorcerer walked to the center of the room unaided and without faltering. Once again he held the gold disc over his head. He closed his eyes and began to whisper a chant. Some of what he said resembled Chinese, but most of it was in the strange, guttural language he'd used earlier. On and on the sorcerer chanted. His words were soft at first, but gradually gained in volume. Then, like cracking thunder, the sorcerer's words suddenly boomed across the chamber. His voice was strong and commanding. It echoed and rumbled as if its source were supernatural and not human. With a loud snapping noise, the gold disc lit up. Out of it swirled a cloud of silver-blue light. The radiant cloud billowed and churned as if it were alive. It washed over the sorcerer's hands, arms and head. The luminance continued to spiral down his body. Once it had encompassed him fully, the light started to undulate in concert with the rhythm of the sorcerer's chanting. The candles in the room flickered and their flames turned blue. Then, as if the light had been sucked from the room, everything darkened. The cloud, however, glowed even more intensely. When the sorcerer opened his eyes again, they were as white as new fallen snow. This sent a chill running through me. A crackle of blue lightning suddenly shot from the disc. Before I could even think to move, it struck me in the chest. I felt no pain as the bolt penetrated my body. I began to notice an odd tugging sensation. It felt as though something was being pulled from my breast, ripped from me. I was forced to reposition my feet to keep my balance. Like hands grabbing at me from within, my chest began to feel tighter.

The light withdrew from me at last and slowly returned to the disc. Held captive within the light was a churning dark cloud blacker than a starless night, blacker even than the ogre's pit. I could feel a powerful malevolence radiating from the darkness. It was old and bitter. The tightness I felt in my chest became an oppressive weight. It grew more difficult for me to breathe, as if someone were sitting on my chest. A terrible chill swept over me and I gasped for air. My blood became like ice in my veins.

Was what I felt the old witch's hate given substance?

Straining, I forced myself to look away.

As the dark cloud was drawn into the disc, the silver-blue light faded and the room's normal light returned. I was again able to breathe freely and the warmth returned to my body. Touching the spot on my chest where the light had struck me, I found no burn mark. I wondered what had just happened. Had the old man really lifted the curse?

The old sorcerer stood where he had been when it all began, but now his head was lowered and his shoulders sagged heavily. He was visibly tired and breathed in great, labored heaves. I went to him to see if he was all right. As I did, the old man looked up.

"You now have…two, perhaps…three nights without the curse to burden you," the old sorcerer labored to say. Once more his face showed the signs of his age. Wrinkly sags of drooping skin hung from his cheeks and neck. His movements were sluggish and weak. The rejuvenating effects of the gold disc, it seemed, were only temporary.

"This night you will walk as a man. Best not to waste this boon I've provided you." The old sorcerer's voice was gruff and his tone scolding. His earlier demeanor had returned along with his aged appearance.

"If it is as you say, then I sincerely thank you." I offered the sorcerer a low bow in gratitude.

He struggled as he hobbled past me and pushed aside the arm I had offered him in aid. The ornery cuss walked back to the table and his cane.

Hurrying ahead of him, I brought the cane to him. The old ingrate snatched it from my hand without a word of thanks and made his way back to his chair. Sitting himself down, he asked deridingly, "What will you do now, Kang Goo-shu? Continue wandering about aimlessly? Or will you seek to make a new life for yourself?"

"What sort of life can I have?" I responded as I helped him sit. "I'm still cursed. Even after your spell I'll still be a chicken most nights. Tell me, how a person can lead a normal life with that hanging over him?"

I didn't expect to receive an answer. Not waiting for one, I went to the wall where my duffel bag sat. Into it I placed the glow stone that I'd been carrying in my sash. Then, tucking Wolf Whacker under my arm, I made ready to leave.

"Seek a release from your curse," the old sorcerer said abruptly. "Reverse it totally and you can have the normal life that you desire."

"As I said before, that is what brought me here. But you are the one who told me that the Mang-Wi, who created the magic that curses me, are all gone. What is there for me to do? To whom can I turn to for help?"

The old sorcerer flashed me a wily smile. "In this matter, we may again be of assistance to one another."

I frowned skeptically. "How?" I asked, letting the duffel bag fall from my shoulder.

"This disc," the sorcerer said, holding the gold disc up in the palm of one hand, "is but one of five magical objects that were left behind by the Mang-Wi. Separately, each is incredibly powerful. However, individually, they are unable to reproduce in total, the grandeur of what the Mang-Wi's magics could accomplish. But if they were united..." the sorcerer paused. He could see that I was following where he was going with this.

I caught in his eyes a trace of the same wicked glint he'd had when he'd proposed that I get rid of the ogre. I was again reminded of my mischievous kid brother. But was it just mischief I saw in his eyes, or was it something else? I remained skeptical.

"So you are saying that if brought together, these objects would be awesome and powerful and capable of ridding me totally of the curse?"

"Right you are on all counts, young man. If I had all five objects, I could remove the chicken curse from you fully. Does this not interest you?"

This was too good to be true. There had to be a catch.

"Will retrieving these items require me to fight any more ogres?" I asked.

The sorcerer shrugged.

"Well?" I pressed, insisting on a more definite reply.

"That I cannot say. What I can tell you for certain is that there will be dangers to face on this quest. The four remaining objects are hidden somewhere in the other towers. Whether they're guarded or not, I don't know."

"That's right! You mentioned before that there were other towers. Tell me about them."

"Originally there were twelve. This is the fourth tower that I've discovered. The other three were in ruins. They'd been destroyed long ago, brought down by either earthquakes or fires. I searched the rubble, but came up empty. None of the magical objects had been hidden at those sites. This gold disc is the first of the Mang-Wi artifacts that I've managed to find. It has reconfirmed my belief that the other four still exist."

"Could someone else have found them? You did say that people had been searching for the objects for a long time."

"No!" the old sorcerer said emphatically. "There's no chance of that."

"But how do you know?" I asked.

There was a short pause as the sorcerer chose his words. When he did answer, his voice was soft and distant. "I would know if the others had been activated. This would have revealed their locations to me," he said, referring to the gold disc, which he now cradled in his lap. He stared at the disc's reflective surface a moment and stroked it as one would a cat. "Its connection to the other artifacts is strong," he added. The old man fell silent. For a long while, he continued to stare blankly at the disc. As I watched him, I grew more and more disturbed. The old sorcerer was mesmerized by the object. His full attention seemed to have been drawn into it. I wondered if this was a result of continued contact with the disc. Whatever the reason, it was unsettling. Then, as if snapping awake from a daydream, the sorcerer shook his head and looked up. He saw the bewildered expression on my face and realized that he'd gotten too weird. The old man turned hostile. Scowling at me, he cleared his throat and said, "Remove from that vapid little mind of yours any concern you have that the other objects might have already been discovered. They haven't been! They're out there, waiting to be found."

"Okay, okay, fine," I said, raising my hands in placation. "So, what about the other eight towers? Are they still intact and do you happen to know where they are?"

The sorcerer's temper subsided. He leaned forward in his seat, "I don't know what condition the other towers are in, but I do have some ideas as to where a few of them are located. Over the years,

my research has revealed that two are situated on distant mountains. A third may be hidden deep in the wooded hills far to the southwest. A fourth I am certain sank into the Eastern Sea over a thousand years ago. As for the others, I have no specific information."

"On top of mountains, deep in the woods, under the ocean!" I said excitedly. "Good grief! How do you expect me to reach all of those places?"

"The towers are not inaccessible. You're young and strong... of body, at least, if not mind. You'll find a way," the old sorcerer replied. "Now, regarding your earlier concern about danger, I must warn you to remain constantly on your guard. The ogre that you defeated was drawn to this tower by the mystical energies of the disc. Other monstrous things may well have gravitated to the towers containing the remaining objects."

"Other monstrous things? What do you mean by that?" I asked, although honestly I wasn't sure that I wanted to hear the answer.

"I told you, I can't say. There are so many nasty things left in the world. Remnants of the Dark One's forces still roam these lands. Who knows what might have been drawn to the towers?" he said indifferently.

My instincts told me not to trust the old snake. He was holding something back. After sixty-nine years of research and searching, this couldn't be all he knew.

Sensing my apprehension, the old sorcerer said, "I doubt taking up this quest will be any more risky than spending each night for the rest of your life as a tasty chicken."

I had to admit the old guy did bring up a good point. As a chicken, I had run afoul of foxes, wolves and people. What little good fortune I'd had in surviving these encounters would eventually run out and someday, someone or something would eat me. It was an unsettling thought, but true. Whether I went on this quest or not, I'd be living a dangerous life. But the curse was not of my choosing; taking on this challenge was. I weighed the consequences carefully.

The old sorcerer saw that I was on the verge of making up my mind and quickly interjected a final incentive. "If you agree to go on this quest, I can offer you some protection."

"Oh really? What protection might that be?" I said dubiously.

"Give me that runty twig you're carrying and I'll show you."

"Runty?" I objected. "Wolf Whacker's not a runty twig, you dried up old fruit. It's helped me fend off wolves and bullies."

"What a heroic little stick it is," the sorcerer mocked. He thrust his hand out, pressing me to hand over the staff.

Reluctantly, I did.

"Naming your puny weapon," he said with contempt. "How sentimental young people can be."

Rising from the chair, the sorcerer took Wolf Whacker to the table and set it down. Looking back at me, he said, "Watch well, Boy. I shall transform this toy of yours into a true weapon, one remade through magic. It shall be unbreakable and will possess the ability to expand to whatever length you command."

"Yeah, sure," I laughed. "I'd be more than happy if you didn't turn it into a noodle or make it crooked."

The sorcerer ignored my remarks. Turning back to the table, he looked down at the staff. Holding the gold disc over his head, he again began to chant in the unknown language. Suddenly, a fiery ray of blue light burst forth from the disc and struck the staff. Wolf Whacker began to glow with a pure white radiance as blinding as that of the sun. I turned my head away and shielded my eyes with my arms. What was that wizard doing to my staff? In the blink of an eye, the light vanished.

Hesitantly, I opened my eyes again. I had to blink several times to clear away the red spots that I was seeing.

Looking at the table, I saw that Wolf Whacker was unchanged. Had the sorcerer's spell worked? Had it done anything at all?

While my staff didn't seem the worse for the experience, the same couldn't be said for the old sorcerer. His skin was pallid and his breathing labored. A sheen of sweat glistened on his creased brow. He leaned heavily on the edge of the table for support. The disc was on the table in front of him. Earlier the disc's magic had given the old sorcerer strength and vitality. Now the old man seemed to have neither. The benefits he received from the disc clearly diminished each time he drew upon the object's powers.

Concerned for him, I ran and fetched the sorcerer his chair. After helping him into it, I then grabbed the disc off the table and offered it to him. "Here," I said, pushing it towards him. "Use it to make yourself strong again."

The old sorcerer shook his head weakly. In a hoarse voice, he replied, "No…dare…not. Too…soon."

I didn't understand his refusal; nevertheless, I returned the disc to the table. I watched the old guy carefully, afraid that he might drop dead on the spot. After a few moments of attentive watching, I was relieved to see the old man's strength return. When he'd caught his breath sufficiently, he pointed to the staff. "Pick it up and give it a try," he said weakly.

"Are you sure you're all right?" I asked.

"I'll be fine in a few minutes if you'll just stop hounding me with foolish questions and do as I say. Try out the staff." The old man shoved me in the arm to get me to move.

I held my place and looked at the old sorcerer. The color had returned to his face and his breathing was steadier than it was earlier. He looked much better. I decided to do as he said.

Going over to the table, I lifted Wolf Whacker up and held it in my hands. It didn't feel any lighter or heavier than before, but there was something different about it. I felt a force pulsating within it, coursing through the wood. As I gripped the staff, I sensed that I was somehow connected to the energy. The sorcerer's spell had done something after all. This was exciting. I was eager to try out the staff's abilities.

"How far will it expand?" I asked anxiously.

Having regained most of his sour vinegar, the old sorcerer brusquely replied, "I don't know! This is magic, not science. I can't give you exact measurements. Go play with it and learn for yourself."

I decided to test the staff's strength first. Looking around the room, I chose one of the wood columns for my target. Each column was as broad as my shoulders. A hard whack with the staff against something so sturdy would ordinarily snap the weapon in two. That

had better not happen, I thought to myself. If it did, that old sorcerer would be getting an earful from me.

Holding Wolf Whacker with both hands, I wound up and swung it as hard as I could at the column. The pole struck the beam with an ear-splitting "crack." The impact reverberated through my hands and up to my shoulders. Amazingly, the staff didn't break. Inspecting where the pole had struck, I found that my blow had created a good-

sized indentation in the beam. The surrounding wood was deeply splintered. Wolf Whacker on the other hand was undamaged. I ran my hand along its length, feeling for a dent, but found none. It was unscathed. The staff was as strong as the sorcerer had promised it would be.

I smiled, pleased with my weapon's new resilience.

Looking at the old sorcerer, I saw him smiling. "It's good, isn't it?" he said, gloating over his own success.

"Definitely," I replied with an enthusiastic nod.

"Now test its ability to expand."

"What do I do?"

"Just think it. Picture the staff expanding in your mind and it will do the rest."

Closing my eyes, I silently commanded Wolf Whacker to grow longer. The shaft shuddered in my hands. I opened my eyes to see what had happened. My curiosity was met with immediate disappointment. The lousy staff had barely grown more than a hand's length longer at either end. My expectations had been a lot grander than a nubby little extension. This wouldn't do me any good at all.

"This is it? You old fake! This is worthless," I shouted angrily.

The sorcerer smirked and said, "The power of the staff comes from your thoughts. If the mind doing the thinking is weak and unfocused, then the staff will respond in kind."

"So you're implying that I'm weak minded? Thanks a lot."

"Nice of you to take my words as they were intended. Remember the staff only changes its length, not its thickness. So, when you picture the change in your mind, be precise."

"No problem." I was impatient to try again. I'd show that pompous sorcerer what I could do. I'd control the staff perfectly this time.

Closing my eyes, I concentrated on making the ends of the staff expand until they touched the walls. I envisioned the action in my mind and instantly heard the sharp crack of wood on stone. I opened my eyes. To my amazement, the pole's ends had done more than simply touch the walls. They'd imbedded themselves into the stone blocks. Unfortunately, in so doing, they had also punched holes in a pair of the tapestries. While I regretted this unintended destruction, I was still pleased. Wolf Whacker had performed as I'd commanded.

I looked over at the old sorcerer and said, "Weak mind, huh?"

"Beginner's luck," he sneered. "Keep practicing and maybe you'll learn better control. Right now, however, your weapon is stuck in the wall." The sorcerer pointed to the imbedded ends of the staff. "Concentrate and you can retract it with but a thought. If you wish, return it to is former size, or shrink it to fit into the palm of your hand. You can transform it to a precise length, if your focus is clear enough. And from now on, keep your eyes open for pity's sake. You'll do a much better job of focussing if you're looking."

Accepting the old sorcerer's latest set of instructions, I reached out and took hold of Wolf Whacker. Looking at the staff, I pictured it returning to its original size. I'd barely finished forming the thought when Wolf Whacker shrank before my eyes, conforming to the image of it that I'd formed in my mind. The sorcerer was right. If I thought with clarity and precision, I could control the staff perfectly.

"Here!" the sorcerer shouted.

I looked up in time to see him toss me something. Reaching out, I caught the object in one hand. Examining it, I saw that it was a large leather pouch closed at the top by a drawstring.

"Open it," the old sorcerer said.

Tucking Wolf Whacker under my arm, I opened the pouch and turned it over. Out poured twelve, small, square-shaped pieces of green jade. There were too many to easily hold in my hands. I walked to the sorcerer and sat by his chair. I then laid the jade squares out on the chamber floor to better see them.

"These are really beautiful," I said as I examined the jade pieces. Each square was perfectly cut with clean, sharp edges. Their surfaces were smooth and highly polished, giving them a radiant luster that glistened in the candlelight.

Was this some sort of currency? My eyes widened as I wondered how much all this jade must be worth. Back in my valley, we almost never saw the precious green stone. No one could afford it.

The sorcerer must have know what I was thinking for he yelled at me, "Stop drooling over them, you simpleton. They're not for you to spend."

"Then what are they for?"

"How did you think you were going to find the other towers? Using those hawk-like eyes of yours?" the sorcerer chuckled. He squinted his eyes, mimicking me.

"Ow! That's hurtful," I complained.

In response, the mean-spirited old coot gave a gleeful chortle. Hobbling over to me, the sorcerer plucked one of the squares from my hand and held it up to the torchlight.

"Do you recognize these animals?"

"Animals? What animals?" I leaned forward and squinted to better see the pieces I was holding.

Seeing me do this, the old sorcerer laughed so hard he nearly threw himself into another coughing fit. "By the Pearl Dragon's gold beard, you're as blind as a bat, Boy," he said in between all the hacking and insulting laughter.

I was now well accustomed to ignoring the old man's endless jibes and blew this one off gracefully. My focus was solely on the jade pieces. Holding a couple of them close to my face and squinting, I saw that on one side of each square was carved the picture of a different animal.

The old sorcerer tapped his cane impatiently against the floor to get my attention. "Well, do you recognize the animals or not? You do see them, don't you?"

"Yes, I see them," I said. "And I recognize most of them." I began pointing to the ones that I knew. "This one's a tiger. This one's a dog. Here's a cow and a horse. And this one's..." My lips froze when my finger touched on the carving of a chicken. Passing that piece over, I looked at the next one. The animal was strange to me. "Is that a crab?" I asked.

"Yes, it is. You're not as ignorant as you look," the sorcerer complimented in a backhanded fashion. He tossed back to me the jade piece that he'd been holding.

I caught it and looked at it. "A snake," I said, identifying the animal carved on it.

The sorcerer sat back down in his chair. "All together, there are twelve animals; a different one is etched on each piece of jade. Can you guess what these animals correspond to?" The sorcerer's voice and expression were condescending, as if figuring out the connection was actually supposed to be a challenge for me.

"Of course I do. I'm not dumb. Each animal symbolizes one of the towers," I said.

"Very good, young pig herder." The old man started to laugh, then suddenly grimaced. Slouching forward in his chair, he clutched at his chest and coughed juicily.

I stepped back to avoid being sprayed by the burbles of lung phlegm. I was sure that this was the old grump's karma paying him back for all of his nastiness. After a few tense moments, the coughing fit subsided and the old man straightened himself up again. He looked even more fatigued than before. His eyelids were heavy and his gaze vacant. He could probably have done with a nap, but first, there were things that we still needed to discuss.

"Which one represents this tower?" I asked.

The sound of my voice brought the old sorcerer back to an alert state. Wordlessly, he reached out a trembling hand and took from me the shiniest of the jade pieces. He then turned it between his fingers so that I could see the animal carved upon it. It was the one with the rabbit. The sorcerer then dropped the piece back into my hand.

I held the jade square close to my face. For the first time, I noticed that it wasn't the jade's smooth surface that made it shine, but rather, there was a yellow/green light, coming from within it. Comparing it with the other pieces, I saw that each glowed, but to a far lesser extent and only along certain edges. This was more mystical weirdness. In a flash of insight, I made the connection. The rabbit jade represented this tower. Its glow was brighter and even throughout the square, while the other pieces only glowed along certain edges or at a particular corner. I picked up one of the other squares and examined it. Looking at the picture side of the jade, I saw that only its top right corner glowed. I turned the piece over in my hand. As I did, the glow moved as well. No matter which way I turned the square, the glow always pointed in the same direction. I concluded that the glow pointed the way to the jade's respective tower. The brightness of the glow had to indicate how close one was to the tower.

"That rabbit jade piece will lead you back here," the old sorcerer said.

"Yes, I figured it out. The glow of the jade serves a purpose," I said confidently. "It indicates the direction and proximity to a particular tower."

The old sorcerer's eyes widened. He presented me with an almost genuine smile. "Kang Goo-shu, my boy, you do surprise me. Yes, you're exactly right. How observant. The glow does indeed indicate the direction and proximity of a specific tower."

The sorcerer's mood darkened. He became serious. "Now listen carefully to what I'm about to say." The old sorcerer shifted in his seat. His face was very stern. "These jade pieces are the only hope you have of finding the other towers. They are unique and irreplaceable. Guard them with your life and speak of what they represent to no one. There are dark forces out there seeking the same treasures that we do." The sorcerer again coughed and hacked violently. This time the fit lasted only a moment. The old man recomposed himself and finished his warning. "Be wary and suspicious of everyone, Boy."

"Wary of what specifically? You're being too vague. It'd be helpful if you started coughing up a little more information and a lot less lung gak," I told him as I wiped a warm chunk of his spew from my chin.

In a huff, the old sorcerer cocked his head to the side and turned his chin up to ignore me. "You've been told what you need to know. Just be on your guard," he said tersely.

These "dark forces" were no joke to the old guy. He was afraid of them, whatever they were. He also knew more about them than he was telling me. I wasn't going to stand by and let him browbeat and bully me into going on this quest blind. Whether he wanted to or not, the old sorcerer was going to tell me what he knew.

"Look, Mister, if you want my help, you'd better tell me something about these dark forces you're going on about. What am I getting myself into?" I demanded.

The old sorcerer blew aside the seriousness of my question with a casual wave of his hand. "I can give you no specifics," he said indifferently. "All I know is that there are others seeking the magics of the Mang-Wi. Some of them are ruthless. They would do anything to get their hands on the magical objects. So I repeat, be on your guard and trust no one. Now ask me no further questions about this. I can tell you nothing more."

"Can't? Or won't?" I wondered to myself.

Looking back at me, the old sorcerer added, "One final thing, Kang Goo-shu, you must find the four objects and return with them to me here before noon on the fifteenth day of the tenth month," the sorcerer added.

"What? But that's just over four months from now. How am I going to go traipsing up and down the length and breadth of the land in such a short period of time?"

"Find a way," the sorcerer insisted flippantly.

"Then you'd better provide me with a pair of magic wings; otherwise, what you're asking is impossible."

The old sorcerer's words took on a threatening undertone. "Let me tell you something that might help to put speed in your step. If you fail to return with all four objects within the time I've specified, I'll be unable to perform the incantations and remove the chicken curse. The full power of the objects can only be unleashed when they are brought together, and then, only during a total solar eclipse. Such an eclipse shall occur at noon on the day I've stated. If the decanting spell is not cast on that day and at the precise moment of the eclipse, you'll remain cursed, probably forever."

"That's a very motivational speech, but it still doesn't solve the problem of how I'm going to cover such a great distance in so short a time."

The sorcerer forced his shriveled lips into an awkward smile and said, "All right then, I'm sure this'll be of help to you." He leaned in closer and bent down. Reaching to the floor, he picked up the jade piece with the carving of a rat upon it. Then he took the snake piece. He dropped both of these into the pouch he carried at his side.

I stared at the old man. "What are you doing?"

Holding my gaze he said, "These are two of the towers that I've already found. You needn't search them." The old sorcerer then plucked the horse jade from the pile on the floor. "I've been to this one as well. None of the magical objects were hidden within it either. However, these remaining towers," he said, indicating to the nine jade squares still on the floor, "with the exception of this tower as represented by the rabbit jade, must be sought out and searched. This leaves you only eight towers to find instead of twelve. You're already a third of the way finished. Isn't that nice?" The sorcerer flashed me a broad grin that once again showed off his unclean teeth. "If you're lucky, the four Mang-Wi artifacts may be found in the very first four towers you reach. That thought should lift your spirits."

"Not really. Need I remind you, I fell under a chicken curse? How lucky could I be? It's more likely that the four objects will be in the very last tower I search."

"That could well be, but that's your problem, not mine. It's all up to you from this point on," the sorcerer said frankly.

I mulled over everything I'd been told. Seeking out and searching the remaining eight towers would be a tall order. I'd be pressed for time. Still, if it meant gaining my freedom from this curse, then it was worth trying.

"How will I identify these magical objects when I see them? Do you know what they look like?" I asked the sorcerer.

Without a word, he rose from his chair and took from my hand one of the jade squares I was holding. The sorcerer proceeded with the square to the table where earlier he'd set down the gold disc. I followed him to the table, curious as to what he would show me. The old sorcerer held the jade square over the disc. I watched as the jade began to glow strong and bright. It shone even more brilliantly than did the rabbit piece. As the sorcerer brought the jade closer to the disc, its yellow/green radiance burned a pure, incandescent white. The brightest star in the heavens couldn't match it.

"Hold any of the squares next to an object that you suspect of being one of the Mang-Wi artifacts, and it will glow like this. Assuming you're right, of course." The sorcerer tossed the jade piece back to me and returned to his seat.

Lowering himself into the chair with a loud grunt, the old guy snorted, "I've made things so simple, even you should have no trouble succeeding."

I had everything I needed to begin my search. However, for the sake of my curiosity, there were still a few questions that I wanted answered before I set off.

"We both know why I am doing this and what I hope to get out of it, but what's in it for you — greater magical powers? Are you hoping to learn the lost spell that would re-grow hair on that pasty, bald head of yours? Or are you after a charm to create a new and more pleasant personality for yourself? Whatever your motives are, I doubt they're respectable."

"You misjudge me," the old sorcerer said, playing the part of the wounded innocent. A far too benign smile slithered across his face as he said, "If you must know, all I want is my youth. As you've pointed out so rudely and so often, I'm old — very old, in fact. My life is nearing its natural end. On my own, I couldn't hope to complete this quest in the short time that I have left. My tired old legs would never take me so far. Nor am I so naive as to think that I might live long enough to try during the next full eclipse, twenty-three years from now. That's why I'm forced to rely on an ignorant wretch like you. Your youthful energy and physical skills make you the perfect tool for my needs."

"Wow! Such flattery. I think I may blush. I really appreciated the tool comparison," I said sarcastically. "So it's not just my problem after all, is it?"

The old sorcerer didn't answer, but the frown on his face was satisfaction enough.

"Don't worry. I'll do my best for both our sakes. You can count on that," I assured him.

Neither of us trusted the other any farther than we could throw this tower. That didn't matter. We didn't have a choice. For me, the sorcerer's plan was my best chance at removing the chicken curse permanently. To the crusty old goat, I was his only hope for a longer life. We needed each other and I figured that would keep the risk of betrayal low for now.

Placing the jade squares back into their leather pouch, I used its drawstrings to secure it to my sash. I next gathered up my duffel bag and Wolf Whacker. As I did, I asked the old sorcerer another question that had been on my mind. "By the way, what's behind that magically sealed door on level four? You know the one that you failed to say anything about?"

The old sorcerer showed no indication of being flustered by the question. Without hesitating, he answered, "That was where the black box containing the disc had originally been stored," he said, casually. "I penetrated the door's mystic barriers and removed the box to the dining chamber for later study. The ogre's arrival interrupted my plans. The room on the other side of the door that you speak of is empty now. It's of no importance."

I nodded as if I believed him. His explanation had a strong thread of plausibility to it, but I just didn't trust the old fox. He was sneaky and secretive by nature. He'd had plenty of time to conjure up a good explanation. His answer still didn't explain why he hadn't mentioned any of it before sending me off. Besides, I remembered the last time the old man had claimed something was unimportant. In that instance, the item turned out to be the gold disc. The old sorcerer's track record for being forthcoming was as poor as my eyesight. Even if he weren't lying outright, he was most certainly omitting something. There was no way to verify my suspicions without checking out the room for myself. That of course would have to wait. For now, I had a quest to begin and one final question to ask.

"Before I go, sir, would you please share with me your name?"

The old man's face twisted into a rigid frown. His wrinkles grew so deep that they became like chasms etched into his face. I knew my question was impolite. It was rude for a young person to ask an elder for their name. The right to offer up their name was totally at the elder's discretion. The old sorcerer had no obligation to tell me his. Under the circumstances, however, I believed that I had a right to know. I would be the one risking my life in this venture. I was entrusting my future to this old guy. I should at least be allowed to know who he was.

The old sorcerer shifted uneasily in his seat before responding, "Very well, as improper as your request is, I'll share with you my name. I am called Cha Young-shyu."

I bowed deeply to him, "Cha Young-shyu, Sir, I shall see you before the fifteenth day of the tenth month." Without further words, I left the observatory.

It was still rather early in the morning when I departed the tower. After passing through the invisible barrier again, I turned and looked back. The tower had disappeared. Picking up a stone, I tossed it at where the tower had been. The stone passed through only empty air. I had been right. On this side of the barrier, the tower did not exist.

It wasn't just invisible. It was gone, as if it had never been. All that remained was the empty quiet of the clearing. A prickly feeling at the back of my neck, nevertheless, caused me to look up. My gaze went to where I imagined the balcony of the tower to be. I felt certain that I was being watched. I imagined the old sorcerer looking down on me. Was he laughing to himself? Did he believe that in me he'd found the perfect patsy? Did he think that I was too young and too simple-minded to know what dangers lay ahead? If so, he was wrong. Since being forced to leave my village, I'd discovered that the world was far bigger than I'd ever dreamed. I would be cautious and ever on my guard as the sorcerer had warned. I'd also be suspicious of him. He'd proven himself deceitful more than once.

I descended the hill and still had most of the day left for traveling. I couldn't waste a minute of it. Somewhere out there were the four remaining magic objects and the eight towers in which they might be located. With any luck, I wouldn't have to search all the towers to find what I was seeking.

Opening the pouch of jade squares, I poured them into my hand. I looked at each of them. The monkey jade had the strongest glow and it was pointing north. That's where I'd head first.

I didn't know what dangers I might encounter during the course of my travels: ghosts, ogres or demonically possessed frogs. It didn't really matter. I'd already discovered that the road of my life was destined to be fraught with hazards, quest or no quest. But I was Kang Goo-shu, champion of the Eastern Village. I was armed with an enchanted staff and my peerless fighting skills. Nothing would stop me.

The Legend of Goo-shu: Journal 2

Goo-shu's quest to rid himself of the chicken curse has begun. The search for the four remaining Mang-Wi artifacts takes him north, where new enemies, new friends and new frights await. He is joined along the way by an unexpected ally, a kindred spirit from his past. Even with this new friend's help, the search for the next tower will not be easy. From the Nine Dragon Falls to the Mountain of the Heavenly Goddesses, Goo-shu must battle for his life. As he struggles to survive fire and beasts, cutthroats and Koguryo soldiers, he will discover that being a chicken boy may be the least of his worries. At the end of this leg of the quest, Goo-shu will come face to face with a creature both dark and terrible, a predator that slays all it encounters. Will Goo-shu and his new companion be strong enough, brave enough and crafty enough to defeat it? Will their efforts lead to the discovery of a second magical object? Or will death be the adventurers' reward?

Fall 2004

For more information about

The Legend of Goo-Shu,

visit us at:

www.gooshu.com